The Curse that Bites

A HEX ON ME MYSTERY
BOOK FOUR

KENNEDY LAYNE

THE CURSE THAT BITES

DEDICATION

Jeffrey & Cole—This year's Halloween outdoor decorations will finally include a vampire...it's going to be epic!

A cloud of bats is whipping up an exciting whodunit in the latest installment in the Hex on Me Mysteries by USA Today Bestselling Author Kennedy Layne...

Lou and the gang become stranded when their brand-new RV breaks down in the middle of Podunk, USA. They soon realize that their arrival in this tiny town might not be by happenstance. Their situation becomes exceptionally dire when Lou has another premonition of murder...this time, the victim is one of their very own group!

A garlic necklace might be an appropriate accessory to bring along for this evening's entertainment, as this tale promises to be as wickedly sharp as the tip on the end of a wooden stake!

Chapter One

T HE FIRST SNOWFALL of the winter season was always
so serene. Not the meager flurries that left the
illusion of a slight dusting on the ground, but the real,
heavy snowfall that blanketed a good six to eight inches
over the landscape as far as the eye could see. That type
of cover was accompanied by a quiet peace associated
with a sudden stillness of nature that only moments
before seemed to rage with the ravages of fall. That
particular type of splendor wasn't revered enough these
days.

"Maybe it's because we're stranded in the middle of
nowhere during a snowstorm with the temperature well
below freezing," Orwin muttered in frustration from
underneath the hood of our brand-new RV. It was a
wonder he could see anything through those black-
rimmed glasses of his that were now spotted with melting
snowflakes. Granted, the luxury camper had been
previously owned by a movie production company for a
short while, but it was still new enough that the
odometer showed almost nothing but the miles we had

put on her ourselves. We shouldn't have had to worry about being stranded in the mountains of West Virginia. "I can't find a thing wrong with this engine, Lou."

That's what I had been afraid of, especially since the tranquility of these mountains had a threatening undertone that was palpable in the surrounding forest. The serenity I had enjoyed so much now seemed to be nothing more than a thin façade.

What—or who—was taking cover in the nearby woods?

"There doesn't seem to be a house around for miles," I hazarded a guess, carefully scanning the lower portion of the mountain below us for any sign of chimney smoke. I wasn't referring to a supernatural vision of any sort, either, but it was hard to see a long distance through the falling snow. "Well, it's not like we have a choice. Go ahead and cast a spell to get us moving along. I don't want to sit here and burn up what's left of our thirty-five gallon propane fuel supply for the two heaters. That could leave us in a real pickle. The magical fix should last us long enough to reach the next small town where we can have a mechanic take a look at it. I'm going to take a little walk around. I won't go too far."

I didn't give Orwin a chance to argue with me. We'd been traveling for the last two weeks in search of an elusive medium who could contact our ancestors. It was a bit extreme, but my current predicament wasn't the run-of-the-mill witchcraft dilemma one would expect of a young witch fresh from teaching my third year at a mid-level college. Everyone in our small group had been a bit on edge lately, and no amount of chocolate or coffee had helped lighten the mood in the last two weeks. I should know, considering I had probably ingested a bit more than my fair share of caffeine these past few days.

There was a reason that our nerves were frayed more than usual, and it all led back to Ammeline Letty Romilda, the infamous Lich Queen. We'd all previously believed that she'd been nothing but an urban legend. If we had been tempted to believe at all, it had been just another long line of stories to keep children in line throughout the many covens across the world—a wicked witch who had somehow harnessed enough dark energy to make herself immortal. It was necromancy in its most evil and malevolent form. It had made great fodder for campfire stories.

Unfortunately, Ammeline's existence had been no myth, much to our vexation.

I should know, because I'd met her foul presence face to face. Evil incarnate was the only description that fit the Lich Queen. It radiated from her very core. The result of that confrontation had left me hexed in the most terrible fashion, which was the reason I needed to speak with my ancestors. Maybe they had the answers I sought to make myself whole once again.

My name?

Tempest Darcinean Lilura.

Quite a mouthful, but then again, so were all the other names of my elders and their progeny.

I just so happened to be a descendent of a family line that was connected to the original Salem witch coven, which I'd happily walked away from at the tender age of eighteen. Considering the position I now found myself in, that had probably been the wisest decision I'd made in my twenty-eight years of life. There was no need to focus on the past, though, when the present was bestowing us with so many wonderful new complications.

I focused on my surroundings, trying to discern why the elements around me were so unnaturally muted. The trees and wildlife of the wilderness should have been causing a balanced hum of energy with the passing of the storm. It would have sounded similar to a guitar string after having been plucked, yet it was like nature didn't have a voice here. All I could pick up was a muffled vibration, similar to when one used their fingers to plug their ears.

Something in these snow-covered woods was smothering the natural energy mechanisms of Mother Nature.

It didn't help that it was becoming difficult to tell if it was still daytime. The snowstorm had blocked out much of the sky with its eternal grey presence, allowing big fluffy flakes to slowly drift down from above as the initial force of the storm ebbed away. Maybe two inches had already fallen, but it was enough to cause hazardous conditions on roads that remained unplowed. It wouldn't be long before the wind picked up and made it hard to see our hands in front of our faces.

Miss Lilura, are you searching for something in particular? It's quite cold out here. We could be back in the RV enjoying a warm spot of cream and curled up next to the electric heater while Mr. Cornelia gets the main drive system under the bonnet back up and running.

That English accent had come from Pearl Pippa Allifair, our resident familiar. She was a sleek white feline who had a thing for etiquette and categorically refused to call me Lou, like everyone else had learned to do. *Everyone else* consisted of Orwin Cornelia, Piper Allifair, and Knox Emeric. Fortunately, or rather unfortunately, we all had our own reasons to search for Ammeline. I was just glad to have them by my side, because I wasn't sure what I'd do without them if we succeeded in finding our mutual evil antagonist.

That's a nice sentiment, dear hexed one, but you'll not find Ammeline out here in the cold. She's most likely in some faraway frightful cave, dancing sans clothes around the flickering flames of a roaring fire while repeatedly chanting some arcane incantations that invoke the most heinous sort of dark magic. Not a sight that I would want to see, dear hexed one. Goodness, no!

Pearl could also read our thoughts, which didn't lend us too much privacy. I'd gotten pretty used to her abilities, though, seeing as Orwin had a similar gift. Piper was our healer, and Knox...well, Knox's run-in with

Ammeline had left him with the most onerous form of lycanthropy.

Our resident werewolf is not just any ol' werewolf, Miss Lilura. The much larger proportions of Mr. Emeric's massive frame comes from the Canis Lupus Occidentalis, originating from the McKenzie Valley variety. Very impressive, if I do say so myself.

"Don't you feel that?" I asked softly, not wanting to discuss Knox at the moment.

Pearl seemed to have cultivated the idea in her head that there was more to my friendship with Knox than there actually was in reality.

There wasn't.

The truth was simple, really. We had both been cursed with dreadful hexes that resulted in our mutual goal—finding the source of Ammeline Letty Romilda's immortality and destroying it. There was nothing more to our relationship than our one specific agenda.

One thinks thou doth protest too much, I believe.

Not wanting to get sidetracked for the millionth time, I cautiously surveyed our surroundings. If I didn't know any better, I'd swear someone was watching us through the trees.

"We're not alone," I murmured, tensing when I couldn't detect a location from which someone's stare weighed heavily on my senses.

Pearl was capable of invisibility, which was her current state. I could sense when she was by my side and hear her thoughts. At the moment, she remained silent as she took heed of my warning. She was most likely scouring the tree line with her own exceptional sight. I held my breath in hopes that she would be able to pinpoint the area that I couldn't seem to detect in the grey shadows.

A quick look back at the RV didn't reveal much, but Orwin must still be casting an incantation on the large diesel motor of the Volvo 780 chassis the RV was built on. I had to wonder what was taking him so long. Piper was safely inside the luxury home on wheels, and Knox hadn't been but a few miles behind us. It shouldn't be long until the purr of his engine cut through the peculiar stillness. His arrival would also bolster our defenses and provide a supernatural sight and sound detection capability far superior to Pearl's.

Fear, Miss Lilura. That's what I sense, and it's causing my fur to stand on edge. May I suggest we head back to the RV now? There's always safety in numbers, and we are currently down a team member.

I would have given Pearl a questioning glance in regard to the rather stark adjective she'd chosen to describe the vibe of this mountain, but she still remained invisible to the naked eye. Instead, I took her opinion under advisement. After all, I appeared to any potential adversary to be standing out here all by myself.

Was fear the underlying tenor of the dense forest?

A gust of bitter cold wind wove its way through the foliage as if to supply me with an answer. I'd made sure I had the proper winter gear on before stepping out of the RV to help Orwin, but there was no keeping the piercing draft from hitting my face full on. I tried to adjust my scarf, but it was of barely of any use.

A warning from the mother, perhaps?

"Go on back with the others," I suggested quietly to Pearl before glancing down the snow-covered, winding road. The falling flakes caught my attention until I was once again looking at the smothered road. What was it about the ground that kept drawing my attention? "Make sure Orwin doesn't need Piper's help in casting that incantation. He should have gotten the drive motor running by now."

Both Orwin and Piper were pros when it came to casting spells, so I didn't expect to be stranded out in the wilderness for very long. Worst case scenario, the RV had its generator. We could survive for several days on the fuel we had on-hand. It wasn't like we'd freeze to death, but I certainly didn't want to be stuck on the side of a mountain with the potential of us being hit by a snowplow. I didn't survive a hex only to be pushed into a ravine by an oversized shovel truck.

Are you finally showing your sense of humor, dear hexed one?

I'll admit to having been a bit testy this past year, but who wouldn't be after being hexed by a Lich Queen? Pearl had made it her mission to get me to lighten up a bit, telling knock-knock jokes at the most inopportune times. I couldn't tell if she had moved the pendulum one way or the other.

Leaders must lead by example, Miss Lilura.

"Yeah, yeah," I muttered, hoping for a change in subject. I lifted my gaze off the blanket of snow on the mountain road toward where there should have been some sign of life. Specifically, headlights from Knox's Land Rover. I didn't like staring into such a grey blank void. "Would you ask Piper to call Knox? Hopefully, she can get cell phone service out here. Knox was still in line at the gas station at the base of the mountain when we pulled out, but he couldn't have been more than a couple of minutes behind us. The good news is that we are topped off on all our fuel tanks, including the propane for the heaters."

My sweet Piper was speaking with our resident werewolf when I left the warmth of the RV. He should be joining us momentarily. In the meantime, may I suggest we both walk back to where Mr. Cornelia is working on the engine before he decides our current troubles are all due to the Machiavellian machinations of little green men?

"In Orwin's defense, this area does seem to have a higher rate of alien abduction claims." I should know, considering I listened to Orwin ramble on about some of the stories he'd researched on the drive from Minnesota to West Virginia. I now knew way too much about aliens and where they liked to stick their probes. "Maybe that's how our medium was abducted. It sure would explain why she left her college and the area before we had a chance to meet her."

You really shouldn't feed into the wizard's conspiracy theories, dear hexed one. It's not healthy for either of you.

I turned against the wind, seeking a bit of respite now that I knew Knox should be reaching us soon. With darkness beginning to settle in, it wasn't like I'd find the cause of my uneasiness anyway. It was best to get the RV up and running as quickly as possible, seeing as we still had another forty-minute drive to reach the year-round all-service campground we'd chosen to spend the night.

"Fine," I relented with a sigh, the warmth of my breath visible as it hit the cold air. "Let's go see what is keeping Orwin from casting that spell. He should have—"

Oh, dear! Here we go again.

My vision suddenly became somewhat blurred, effectively causing me to stop midstride. The hex that plagued me was about to make a grand entrance unique to my curse, and there wasn't a thing I could do to stop the vision from happening. Due to a familiar's ability to connect with the thoughts of other witches and warlocks, Pearl was linked to the ghastly images inside my mind and doomed to perceive my deadly message herself.

I might prefer an alien abduction to these unsettling premonitions, dear hexed one. Hold on to your hat. This one promises to be a doozy!

Chapter Two

I DREADED THESE visions more than anything in the world. You see, Ammeline Letty Romilda had cursed me with premonitions of murders yet to happen. Sometimes the team and I were able to make it to a destination in time to save the victim, and other times we arrived after the fact, only allowing us the ability to bring their killer to justice.

I have a feeling it will be the latter of the two this time around, dear hexed one. We're in the middle of a snowstorm. There is not much that can be done while we're stuck on a high mountain pass.

It was a good thing I had been able to move off to the shoulder just in case Knox came barreling up the road a bit too fast in these weather conditions. I purposefully fell to my knees in the soft snow, not caring that my jeans would get soaking wet. There was no telling how strong the vision would be, and I certainly didn't want to fall and slip down some steep ravine.

One minute I was watching the snow fall in front of me and then next…well, I was inside a log cabin with rays of light shining in from a window shrouded in old, faded yellow curtains. Dust particles floated in the beams as if in slow motion. There was a beautiful river rock hearth without the typical blazing fire, no pictures on the wall, and sparse furniture. It was as if the special getaway home had been abandoned many years ago. There was even a large cobweb in the corner. I was somehow able to turn myself around to face the front door just in time for it to bang open and reveal one of my worst nightmares.

The victims in my premonitions had always been in regard to a stranger, leaving me and the others to try and locate the scene of the crime. We usually inserted ourselves into the lives of the victim's family and friends to help them find closure or to protect the potential victim.

Well, we weren't going to have to travel too far this time around.

The individual in my vision who was bleeding from the neck was none other than a member of our own team. Our very own wizard—Orwin Cornelia.

His black-rimmed glasses were a bit askew as he tried to stem the lone gush of blood escaping from his grip. The panic in his brown eyes was unmistakable, and there wasn't a thing I could do to reassure him that all would be okay as I was all but sucked out of the vision and brought back to the present.

Bollocks! It can't be, dear hexed one!

I managed to push my gloved hands off the ground

and kneel back atop my winter boots just as bright headlights appeared from behind me to illuminate the area through the falling snow. My premonitions usually lasted less than thirty seconds, but this time it had seemed to go on forever.

"Lou?"

I could hear the concern in Knox's voice as he must have quickly shoved his Land Rover into park and all but launched himself out of his vehicle. I could only imagine what he thought at finding me collapsed in the snow on the side of the road, but I'd had a few seconds to fortify myself for the battle ahead.

I would move heaven and earth to ensure Orwin's safety.

We both will, dear hexed one. I might bemoan those conspiracy theories of his, but I've become quite fond of our constant banter.

Knox's brown boots he'd grown accustomed to wearing since his time in the military appeared before me. There was an added bonus to looking at things this low to the ground, because I had finally discovered what had been so odd about the blanket of snow that covered the road and knit its way throughout the trees.

There were no animal tracks in the fresh snow, which wasn't that odd until you looked closer and realized there weren't any tracks underneath the fresh blanket of white, either.

None at all.

"I'm okay," I managed to say, finally able to control the shivers that had settled in.

A spot of warm cream will help heat us right up, dear hexed one. We can compare notes to ensure that your premonition never sees fruition. We'll be able to stop whatever this is from happening. As you well know, we have a battle ahead of us, and it is best we break this gently to Mr. Cornelia. We'll fortify a plan to ensure the alien hunter's safety. He might not like the idea of me sticking to him like glue, but it will be for his own good in spite of his allergies.

No, Orwin wasn't going to like this at all. And now was not the time for weakness, not when one of our own was in danger. I gratefully took hold of Knox's hand as he helped me stand, nodding to him when his dark gaze searched mine for reassurance that I wasn't hurt. Not physically, anyway. The pain of seeing someone I deeply cared about in one of my premonitions was something else entirely.

"Let me guess," Knox said in concern, using his warm thumb to gently brush away a few flakes that had landed on my cheek. He must have left his gloves inside his vehicle. "Another vision?"

Yes, and it was a doozy. I'll leave you to catch our resident werewolf up on the specifics while I go and attach myself to Mr. Cornelia's side. I can't promise I won't come across a bit paranoid after this experiment, but I'm sure it's nothing a spot of warm cream can't mend.

"Yes, and this premonition hits a little too close to

home," I replied to Knox, knowing full well he couldn't hear Pearl. He probably hadn't even known she'd been near me during the vision. "Knox, the victim in my vision was Orwin. He had some type of bleeding injury to his neck, and he somehow managed to find an abandoned cabin out here before he bled out. I'm assuming somewhere on this mountaintop."

"His neck? Well, I might know the reason why," Knox replied grimly, his golden eyes practically glowing as he scanned the ridge of trees that sloped down into an abyss of darkness. "We're in vampire territory, Lou. I could smell that rancid copper scent back at the gas station."

That would explain the muted tones of Mother Nature in the immediate vicinity, the snow void of any animal tracks, and my vision of Orwin clutching his neck. Just as with any other form of supernatural beings, not all vampires were bloodsucking murderers. There were many who were able to control their urges, using blood banks to satiate their thirst.

Unfortunately, it only took one bad apple in the orchard to turn the harvest.

"That nauseating odor seemed to be drifting down from the mountain, but I stayed behind for a few minutes to make sure the little town was clear of any vamps." Knox had dropped his hand from my arm as he continued to peruse the tree line. His vision was unparalleled as a werewolf, just as all of his other senses were heightened to the max. His body heat had all but seared my skin through the thick material of my coat, and my arm was now cold without his touch. "Whoever would establish a lair this far out from civilization is trying to cover their tracks. They're attempting to go undetected."

"Is that why Pearl didn't catch their scent?" I asked, grateful that Knox's headlights illuminated the RV a short distance away. I witnessed Orwin set his hands on top of his head in disbelief. It appeared that Pearl had already spilled the beans, and now Piper was stepping out from the safety of our traveling headquarters. "Why would the vampires need to mask their presence this far from town? Why go to all that trouble?"

"Good question." Knox's tone indicated that he didn't like the possibilities that inquiry left open. Then again, neither did I. "Piper mentioned on the phone that you had a bit of engine trouble. Was Orwin able to get the RV up and running? This storm is picking up faster than anticipated. If we waste any more time, we won't be able to drive up or down this grade."

"I think that's the crux of our dilemma," I murmured, having already weighed our options. They weren't good, and the others weren't going to like my decision. "For whatever reason, someone doesn't want us to leave this mountain."

"Something tells me we aren't going anywhere." Knox regarded me cautiously while the falling snow picked up its pace once again, as if we needed another warning of what hid in the shadows. "I've got to hand it to you, Lou. You don't back down from a fight."

Word to the wise, dear hexed one.

Knox had begun the short trek to where his Land Rover was still parked on the side of the road by the time Pearl had rejoined me to escort me safely back to the RV. He would follow behind until we were able to come up with a strategy to keep Orwin safe while we deciphered more details about my premonition. If I knew with one hundred percent certainty that his imminent death took place on this very mountain, I would do everything in my power to make sure he was far away from here at the appointed time.

"I already know what you're going to say, Pearl." I advanced forward to where Orwin and Piper stood next to the open door of the RV. This perilous situation hadn't been in the cards, but that was usually the outcome with these visions. We'd learned to adapt. "You're going to point out that I should also know when to run away from danger. I'll tell you this—whatever is preying on this mountain hasn't taken us into account."

Run? I would never consider such a thing, Miss Lilura. Retreat and regroup would be more like it. My words of wisdom have more to do with a specific herb upon hearing your discussion with our resident werewolf. I'm not particularly a fan of the pungent bulb, but I believe it's time that we stock up on some garlic...and lots of it, dear hexed one. We're most likely going to need it come morning. Besides, I could do with a spot of Italian for dinner.

Chapter Three

"ORWIN, YOU OF all people should know for a fact that not all of Lou's premonitions come true," Piper said reassuringly, setting a hot cup of coffee in front of Orwin. Unfortunately, the slight tremor in her hand spoke volumes in regard to the comfort she was trying to bestow upon our friend. It also didn't help that he could basically hear all of our thoughts, which were no doubt filled with our own uncertainty and worry. "We have the ability to change the future. We've done it before, and we'll do it again. We'll make sure that you're never left alone, we'll take precautions with various wards and incantations, and we'll also take out the protection crystals that we have in our inventory."

Don't forget the garlic and wooden stakes, my sweet Piper. We're not dealing with mere humans here. It would behoove us to remember that vampires have super strength and speed.

It had taken us close to an hour to drive twenty miles, but we'd finally made it to an overlook that was large enough to fit the fifty-two foot RV, my 4x4 Jeep

Wrangler, and Knox's Land Rover. We'd popped the hitch free of my Jeep and managed to pull it around to the front of the RV, just in case we needed another vehicle besides the Land Rover to cover ground quickly.

The snow had begun to fall harder and faster than anticipated, which had pretty much made the decision for us to stay on this mountaintop. The RV had plenty of room for everyone to spread out and get comfortable while we planned for the inevitable attack. We'd switched back to the generator without any further problems, providing the entire RV with lights throughout and power for all the accessories of a luxury state-of-the-art recreational vehicle.

Orwin had been able to make some improvements during our journey east. I only nodded my understanding when he'd explained how he'd co-opted a high-bandwidth, full duplex non-encrypted channel on a decommissioned geosynchronous mil-star satellite he could tap into anytime we needed it. He also mentioned some omni-directional satellite antenna he'd installed on the roof of the RV, but I'd zoned out by the time he'd finished his sentence. The only thing I'd needed to know was that we had access to the internet.

I could pretty much guarantee that Orwin wasn't thinking about satellites and antennas now. He, Piper, and I had claimed the main dining table, while Knox had pulled over the leather office chair from Orwin's desk so that he had a bit more legroom. He was rubbing his five o'clock shadow the way he did when he was overthinking a tactical problem.

"This is insane," Orwin exclaimed in exasperation. He didn't even bother to reach for his coffee. Maybe we should have popped the cork on something a bit stronger. Then again, we all needed our wits to forestall any impending attack. He'd asked me the same question five or ten times in the last hour, and my answer hadn't changed in those sixty minutes. "Are you one hundred percent positive it was me?"

Oh, yes. There was no mistaking your cowlick, alien hunter. That's quite the mega swoop you have going there.

"Orwin, we're in vampire territory. Knox picked up their scent during our last pit stop, and you were gripping your throat in my vision. We both know what happens to wizards and witches when we're bit by one of them, and it's not pretty." I leaned forward to point at a spot on the map we had laid out on the table. "We're probably another fifteen to twenty miles from the campsite, and another thirty miles from where we think Cassandra Opal Saruman fled to after leaving Minnesota. Once this storm passes, we have a serious decision to make in order to keep you safe while figuring out why a vampire would want to attack us. We're not exactly easy targets, and they'd know that just by observing us for more than a few minutes."

We also needed to deal with the fact that a college girl up and left campus in the middle of a semester after finally agreeing to meet with us. What was even stranger was that she'd fled to a small town in the middle of the West Virginia mountains for no apparent reason. It had taken over a week, but Piper had finally managed to finagle her way into the medium's dorm. She'd stealthily swiped a brush with strands of Cassandra's hair that had been embedded in the bristles. We were then able to cast a locator spell, leading us directly on this path up this particular mountain. It was a little too convenient that we were suddenly running into a pack of assassins now that we were getting close to her location.

I'd repeatedly said before that I wasn't one for coincidences, and I wasn't buying it now, either. Still, I wasn't going to risk Orwin's life in our attempt to locate and speak to Cassandra. We were trying to save lives through our endeavors, not place more at risk.

So, are we splitting up our merry band of sleuths? I'll escort Mr. Cornelia and my sweet Piper far away from here, while you and Mr. Emeric try to figure out why one of the vilest undead creatures would want a taste of our alien hunter. Not to say that you're not delicious, Mr. Cornelia. I'm sure you are, especially with all that sugar you ingest daily. Don't you worry, though. With me by your side, I'll make sure you stick to a healthy diet with plenty of garlic.

"I don't profess to be some type of Ultimate UFC fighter, so my first instinct is to take your advice and leave, Lou," Orwin said, completely ignoring Pearl's well-laid out plan and talk of changing his diet to Italian garlic bread with a side of spaghetti noodles. It was hard to take him seriously when that cowlick of his was a bit askew, especially after Pearl had called attention to it. He'd been running his hand through the thick black strands in worry and innate fear, trying to figure out why Count Chocula would want to feed on him. Who could blame him? "That might not work, though. Have we considered that one of these vamps would just follow me in another vehicle, carrying through with this premonition in a new location? Separating the team might be a very bad idea. It could put all of us at risk."

Quite the conundrum, I must say. Either way, Mr. Cornelia, I will be your sidekick until the typical twenty-four hours have passed before the hexed one's premonition has expired, as it has every other time in our most recent past.

"This is karma at her finest. This is all because I turned Billy's pet hamster into a mouse back in the fifth grade, isn't it?" Orwin slouched against the back of the booth and sneezed. Had he not done so, I would have thought the slight rocking of the RV had been caused by the strong gusts of wind hitting us from the west. Being cooped up inside with a cat and a werewolf was wracking havoc on his allergies. "I knew that day would come back to haunt me."

Karma favors the patient soul, alien hunter.

While Orwin and Pearl continued to debate what drew karma's attention, I took a sip of my coffee. The pumpkin spiced flavor undertone wasn't a surprise, given that Piper loved everything pumpkin. The flavor was oddly comforting, not that I'd let her know that. As it stood, the interior of the RV had pumpkin scents coming from practically every outlet. I'd swear that Piper had bought all the pumpkin spice liquid air fresheners that Yankee Candle had available.

"Piper, have you scried for the medium's location today?"

It was the first time that Knox had spoken since we'd sat down to go over the details of my premonition. He was more of the listening type, taking everything in before offering up his opinion. His rich voice carried loudly throughout the interior of the RV, catching all of us by surprise. Piper had already slid back into the booth beside me after making sure everyone had something hot to drink, including Pearl's spot of warm cream.

It was much needed after that vision, dear hexed one. Those premonitions do take their toll, you know.

"No, I was going to wait until we'd reached the campsite," Piper replied, giving Knox an inquisitive stare, along with everyone else. It was obvious that he had something on his mind, and I was grateful that someone else was thinking along the same lines as me. "The weather might interfere a bit if I try right now. The elements are in a fury, but I'll see what I can do."

Knox nodded his appreciation, reaching out for his own coffee mug that just so happened to have a pumpkin painted on the side. Piper had made herself a cup of tea, and she took it with her when she went to retrieve the items needed to ensure that Cassandra was still at her last known location. Piper scried every day, and the result had always been the same.

I loathe to point this out, Miss Lilura, but the medium could have been made aware of our impending visit and might have arranged for our situation, as it currently stands. This chase we have been chosen to be a part of might very well be skewed in her favor.

"I agree with Orwin. Dividing the group into two is a bad idea," I finally declared, saying aloud what Orwin was already hearing inside of my head. He was probably getting hit with everyone else's thoughts on what the right thing to do was in this sensitive situation, but he would ultimately follow my lead. That type of responsibility weighed heavily on my soul each and every day, but I would lay my life down for each of these people who'd become my family. "In the end, it might not matter what decision we make. Orwin still might end up in that isolated cabin holding the side of his neck. We need to prepare for the worst."

"Ohhhh, this is bad. This is really bad," Orwin whispered, shoving his fingers underneath his glasses so that he could rub his bloodshot eyes. I wasn't sure if that due to fear or his allergies. "I don't belong on the front lines. I'm much more of a support guy. You know what I mean, useful behind a computer screen and all that."

Pearl had known where I was leading this discussion. She'd even begun to silently move her position closer to me before my suggestion finally penetrated Orwin's haze of disbelief. There was no question that he needed to remove the protection spell he'd cast upon himself against Ammeline Letty Romilda. If worse came to worse, Piper needed to be able to save his life.

My moving away from a boiling pot is called self-preservation, dear hexed one. Shall I do the countdown? Three, two, one…

Chapter Four

"OH, NO. No, no, no," Orwin protested vehemently, finally comprehending what I'd truly meant by preparing for the worst. His glasses were now a bit lopsided from rubbing his face as he began to shake his finger in my direction. He'd proven Pearl right with his reaction, but she was already positioned on the back ledge of the booth beside me. "I know what you're suggesting, and there's got to be another way. You know firsthand how long it took for me to locate all the material components for that protection spell. The day will come when we meet up with Ammeline Letty Romilda, and I made sure I was well-protected against her magic so that at least one of us would have the ability to reach the source of her power before she turned us all into slithering reptiles or something just as heinous."

Oh, dear hexed one, now might be the time for a bit of tough love. You'll need to spell this out—no pun intended—a bit clearer for the alien hunter so that he understands the ramifications of his decision.

"It won't matter if you're dead," Knox countered

uncharacteristically, giving us a glimpse of the man he'd been during his time with the Marine Raiders. He usually remained on the sidelines, ever watchful over the choices we made and the eventual consequences of those decisions. It was good to know that he was fully invested in us the same as we were with him. "There are two facts that you need to accept, Cornelia. One, Piper has the ability to heal and cure disease and injuries. Two, you're going to need for her to be able to do her job unhindered when the time comes. It's that simple. Get rid of the warding spell, protection spell, or whatever you want to call your safe space. That's really the only option you have right now—so do what is necessary for your survival or suffer the consequences."

Oh, my. If I weren't a familiar, I might have to give you a run for your money, Miss Lilura.

I shot Pearl a glare that she couldn't mistake for anything else but annoyance.

We must enjoy the little moments in life, for we know not what tomorrow may bring. Have we not covered this topic before? Oh, that's right…we have. Besides, we're safely ensconced inside the RV until the storm passes. In case you didn't know it, dear hexed one, humor is what alleviates the paralyzing side effects of fear. We should thoroughly utilize all the weapons at our disposal.

"Well, your type of humor is not helping me in the least," Orwin criticized in what sounded like pure exhaustion before leaning his head back against the booth in frustration. Maybe his position would help alleviate some of his allergy symptoms. His nose was turning an odd shade of ripe pomegranate red. "There's got to be another way."

Death, but I would hope you would want to avoid what would seem to be a rather permanent solution to a temporary problem.

Orwin was definitely going to need a few moments to get on board with lowering the only defense he had against Ammeline. I completely understood his inner quandary. With that said, Knox certainly hadn't sugarcoated the truth, as Pearl had so thoroughly pointed out. Unfortunately, there really was only one viable choice available.

"It would have made our situation much easier had I seen whoever it was that attacked you in my vision. We weren't that lucky, Orwin, which leaves us with basically no alternatives."

Did you happen to see the fishing poles in the corner of the cabin, Miss Lilura? I'd say the location we are looking for is near a pond or a lake. Once again, I must point out the obvious that Mr. Cornelia should stay far away from any cabin if we all decide to stay together.

Knox and I both leaned forward at the same time, with me scooting closer so that we could slide the map toward us in order to see what bodies of water were close to our location. Pearl had mentioned the twenty-four-hour grace period after my premonition. Usually, the person either fell victim to the impending vision within that time or we somehow managed to change the outcome. I could hear the phantom ticks of the second hand as if there was an antique pocket watch pressed against my ear.

"There looks to be a small lake around a half click from here." Knox pointed toward a spot on the map, while I grabbed a highlighter that Piper had been using to line our route to the campsite. "Here's another."

I began circling the locations where Orwin's attack could possibly have occurred, beginning to make a grid that he should stay far away from until we had more information.

That's easier said than done, Miss Lilura. What if the alien hunter and I are chatting away inside the RV about those little green men of his, only to be forced out by one of the undead creatures of the night? My sweet Piper could cast a cloaking enchantment around our traveling home so that it blends in with our surroundings.

"The vampires living in these mountains couldn't have covered their scent without help," Orwin pointed out, purposefully dodging the decision about his protection ward. "The only reason Knox was able to detect them was due to the direction of the wind at the base of the peak. There are few supernatural servant beings who have the ability to cast a masking spell."

A very odd combination, indeed. It's not an everyday occurrence when a witch or druid team up with a vampire.

I sat back in the booth, handing off the yellow highlighter to Knox. He continued to scan for areas where my premonition might have occurred, leaving me to plan the next twenty-four hours. There was only one objective—keeping Orwin alive.

"That would be nice," Orwin muttered, finally reaching for his coffee. He'd taken an allergy pill out of one of the many bottles he'd placed strategically around the RV. I grimaced at what must have been a lukewarm swallow. "I mean, how hard can it be to find a vampire who apparently kills me while a witch does her best to hide his presence on a mountain that goes on for what must be miles?"

I'm going to assume that was a figurative question, Mr. Cornelia. If not, I actually have the odds of our success, if you care to hear them.

"We might have a bigger problem on our hands," Piper announced rather breathlessly as she rejoined us back at the table. In her grasp was the amethyst that she used when scribing for an object or a person. In this case, our missing medium. "Cassandra Opal Saruman is no longer at our final destination."

Oh, dear. This itty-bitty revelation is about to lead us right into a snowbank, isn't it, my sweet Piper?

"Cassandra's here," Piper confirmed, pointing to the small town on a map that just so happened to be twenty miles away from our little overlook of the mountain. "She's maybe a mile away from the campsite we reserved for the next couple of days. She has to be the one who is helping the vampire stay hidden, but why would she do that?"

Knox finished marking areas on the map where the

cabin was most likely located, pushing the local atlas back into the middle of the table. He clicked the cap into place on the highlighter, but kept the marker in his hand.

"Why would the medium we're searching for team up with a vampire?" Knox asked distractedly, flipping the highlighter over his knuckles in an unconscious gesture. He finally set his golden gaze on each one of us until he came to me, as if he'd reached a conclusion. "I presume it's for protection."

Is our resident werewolf trying to say that Miss Saruman is seeking protection from us? I must say that I'm a bit offended, dear hexed one.

I thought back over the last month, quickly connecting some dots that we'd never even thought to link. Orwin had, by chance, discovered Cassandra's séance video that had been nothing but a sorority prank at the time.

"What if we weren't the only ones to see that video?" I asked, wondering if I wasn't stretching for an answer to suit our needs. "What if someone else reached out to Cassandra?"

Are you wondering if you're beginning to sound like our alien hunter? Not quite, Miss Lilura. I'll be the first to yank you back to reality should that be the case.

"Is it possible that Cassandra went into hiding, all because someone else discovered that the séance she'd hosted had some very real elements?" I put forth the question, having already answered myself. This was no conspiracy, and it all actually made sense. It was also technically good news for us. "The first thing we need to do when this storm lifts is to find Cassandra before whomever else is pursuing her achieves that goal. It's best we convince her that we mean no harm, nor do we want to use her abilities for some dark purpose."

"If I were in Cassandra's shoes, I'd only listen to what we had to say if we promised to help her in some way," Piper added, reclaiming her seat. I shifted to make room for her, making sure I took my coffee cup with me. "There must be a reason she didn't seek shelter in her own coven, which means it's best to offer safety in one of ours."

My sweet Piper, not everyone is as trusting as you. It might take some convincing on our part, especially seeing as we are seeking her out for her special abilities. We want to use her gift as well, regardless if it is to stop the insanity a Lich Queen or not.

I could sense the weight of Knox's stare. He had to be curious as to why I hadn't sought the safety of my own coven after being hexed by Ammeline. It wasn't as if I was hiding anything, but talking about my parents and my former coven wasn't high on my list of favorite topics. Orwin most likely felt the same, especially given the fact that he'd been the first to join me in this hunt for the Lich Queen…and now his life was in danger.

"I'll lower the ward of protection."

Orwin's abrupt declaration had garnered all of our attention, but he was mainly focused on Piper. He pushed up his black-rimmed glasses as if he needed a bit more clarity to witness her reaction.

"Are you sure?" Piper asked gently, clearly searching for a reason for Orwin's change of heart.

"I trust you to save me, Piper." Orwin's admission had been heartfelt. He reached across the table for her hand, which she hesitantly offered after what I could only assume was an internal struggle. The weight of responsibility I usually shouldered alone had settled somewhere in her soul. It wasn't a pleasant feeling at all. "We stick together."

We all murmured our agreement for tomorrow's plan, and it wasn't long before Orwin and Piper vacated the table to remove his warding spell.

"You okay?" I asked Pearl softly, who was still settled on the back ledge of the booth. She hadn't muttered aloud one of her usual quips. Her emerald green eyes had followed Piper as she reached for one of the pestles behind us that we had stored in one of the many cabinets. "You're awfully quiet."

I worry about my sweet Piper, dear hexed one. She's very young to have the responsibility of someone's life in her hands. Yes, it's her gift, but that does not make it any less of a burden.

Pearl was always attempting to lighten our days and nights any way she could, and I certainly hadn't made it easy on her. The weight I'd referred to rested on her shoulders as well. This journey we were on had placed all of us in a very precarious situation. I needed to keep reminding myself that I wasn't the only one carrying around a burden.

There was only one thing left to do.

"A familiar walks into a bar…"

You're learning, dear hexed one. There's hope for you yet.

I chuckled as Pearl stretched her front legs, eventually arching her back before she hopped down from the ledge in order to join Orwin and Piper. It was nice to hear the light tinkering laugh she emitted at the end of my joke.

"I can always shove Orwin into the passenger seat of my Land Rover and not stop until we hit the East Coast. I'm pretty sure that cabin you saw wasn't at the beach," Knox offered up, attempting to ease my concern. I twisted the mug in my hand around and around to give myself something to do, because sitting around and waiting wasn't something I was very good at. "There's got to be some UFO sighting he wants to check out in Jersey."

"I'm almost certain there is, but whatever decision we make might be the path leading Orwin directly to that cabin, and you know it." I shook my head, my intuition telling me that no matter what choice we made…Orwin would still be holding the side of his throat while staggering into that abandoned shack. "We stick together, making sure the Pearl and Piper are right by Orwin's side. He'll just have to up his allergy dose tonight."

Morning couldn't come soon enough. That did leave us in a bit of a quandary concerning sleeping arrangements. Knox didn't like the confinement of the RV, and he usually slept outside underneath the stars in a tent. Well, we weren't in a place for that to happen.

"Looks like you're staying with us tonight."

"That it does," Knox replied, his golden eyes darkening just a bit as he met my gaze.

I'm pretty sure that I wasn't going to have to worry about the temperature inside the RV tonight, especially considering the hot flash that washed over me upon his reply. There was no denying that Knox Emeric had a special appeal that would make almost any woman swoon. I had to remind myself that I wasn't the swooning type, and that one of our own was in imminent danger.

Every single decision I made in the next twenty-four hours could affect Orwin's final moments, and I would do well to remember that fact.

Chapter Five

"I WOULDN'T TECHNICALLY call this a town," Orwin muttered, shoving his hands into the warm pockets of his new goose down winter jacket. He'd been wearing his old one in my premonition, so I'd done my best to begin altering the outcome as much as possible. So far, so good. "Some of these structures are pretty far apart. At best, it's a loose collection of buildings with a post office slash gas station slash hardware store combo."

Fourteen hours had passed before we'd been able to finally make our way into this almost nonexistent town. We'd managed to clear out a path for the RV, the Land Rover, and the Wrangler, all of which had managed to collect six inches of fresh snow that had fallen after we'd sought protection at the lookout area. Once that task had been completed, we drove to the campsite and carved out a spot for the RV and repositioned the vehicles for quick access. There was no time to take the RV to a local garage for service. Besides, we needed a commercial truck mechanic.

That was when the disagreements had begun, though

I hesitated to call them arguments. They were more like difference of opinions.

"They were definitely arguments," Orwin countered wryly, opening the door to the diner. At least, I think it was a diner. The place also seemed to serve the townsfolk as a gas station, a hardware store, and what according to the sign was a post office in the back. The odd scents mixing together proved to be quite interesting. "Emeric can take care of himself, you know."

"That's not the point. Knox shouldn't have gone off into the woods by himself."

I still wasn't sure how he'd convinced all of us that it would be best if he patrolled the mountainside facing the town alone. He'd mentioned being able to search the areas we'd circled on the map for any sign of a vampire's nest without the restrictions of moving by vehicle. Granted, he was right, but that didn't make it the safest alternative for any of us.

"In case you forgot, it's not Knox we need to worry about," Orwin reminded me, pushing up his glasses as a young girl asked if we needed fuel or help checking under the hood. We'd stopped directly in front of the countertop. "We're actually hoping you can help us locate my sister. It's a family emergency, and our cell phone provider doesn't seem to be working in this area."

Orwin's cover story had been brilliant, and he'd even pulled his cell phone out to prove his story. It hadn't taken him long to do his techy thing to give weight to his lie, and what he really wanted to do was show the young girl a photograph of Cassandra he'd saved as a screensaver.

"Oh, that's Cassie. That Jerry's bae."

It was one thing to see Orwin's thin black eyebrow lift at anything he couldn't quite figure out, but it was entirely another to see his reaction to the moniker *bae*. He might be twenty-two years old, but he was definitely an old soul.

"Girlfriend," I translated, wondering how he'd survived three and a half years at college. I turned back to the brunette, who was still studying us warily. "Do you know where we can find Jerry and Cassie? It really is a family emergency."

Had we come looking for Cassandra with any other excuse, I had no doubt we would have been shunned and shown the door. Close-knit communities like this took care of their own, and it sounded as if this Jerry guy had deep roots in the community. Folks who wanted to be left alone out in areas like this learned to leave people to their own business. My plea seemed to work, though, when she called to someone over her shoulder.

"Hal, have you seen Jerry today? He was supposed to stop in to pick up that package from Minnesota." The young girl didn't wait for an answer, but instead turned back around to introduce herself. "I'm Tina. Jerry and I went to high school together before they closed it and moved everything to the next town over. He flunked out of college, but that's where he met Cassie. He's totally crazy about your sister, by the way. Give me a second. Hal's a bit deaf."

It was hard to tell if Tina was giving us the brush-off, thus alerting Jerry and Cassandra that there were two strangers in town asking for their whereabouts. Orwin quickly dispelled my concern, though.

"Hal is in his seventies, but he still runs the mail side of the business—Post Office regulations and all that. He lost a fair part of his hearing a while back." Orwin shared with me what had been on Tina's mind before she'd gone in search of Hal. Orwin shifted his weight back and forth on his black boots, impatient for the other ten hours to pass in my vision's timeframe. "All is good so far. Let's just hope that we can find Cassie before it's too late."

Orwin was talking in code, as agreed upon. Just as werewolves were known for their extraordinary abilities, so were vampires. They had their own collection of talents. They could hear over long distances, though not as far as werewolves. Same with scent, though vampires hungered for the taste of blood and that tended to distract them. We had on our side, however, the ultimate bane of the strongest vampires. Even a weak werewolf could destroy a run-of-the-mill bloodsucker. We had a Mackenzie Valley Werewolf that could obliterate an entire den of Dracula types with very little effort.

We had a clear visual of the diner from our location

by the counter, and it was evident that we'd attracted some attention. If there was a vampire anywhere inside this building, he or she would have heard every single word we'd exchanged with Tina.

As it stood, a man was enjoying breakfast as he made no effort to hide the fact that he was watching us intently with each bite he shoved into his mouth. An older couple was sitting in one of the few booths against the far wall, and a twenty-something year old woman sat by herself while drinking a cup of coffee and reading a book. There only seemed to be one waitress on staff, with a cook at the small grill toward the back of the building.

Vampires survived on blood, but they did eat food and drink ordinary beverages to blend in with society. A lot of what you read or heard over the years regarding the blood-sucking creatures were completely a Hollywood myth…with the exception of garlic and wooden oak stakes. It wasn't that garlic actually hurt them in any way, but the scent did make them somewhat nauseated. A lot of the reeking herb could bring them to their knees for the brief seconds needed to get a running start.

"…thanks, Hal." Tina had her hair pulled up into a messy bun, similar to how Piper wore hers when we were on the road. She shot us a smile. "Jerry and Cassie are up at the fishing cabin, but those roads are usually the last to get cleared after a snowfall like the one we had last night. It's a good thing it wasn't a blizzard, or else we wouldn't have seen them for a week or more."

It appeared I'd gotten quite used to living in the state of Washington after leaving the Salem coven, because I personally believed eight inches of snow qualified to be considered for at least a mini-blizzard. Contrary to popular belief, Washington didn't get that much snowfall compared to West Virginia.

"They'll probably make it to town this afternoon or tomorrow morning." An older man stepped out from behind the divider, his sharp blue eyes taking me and Orwin in with intense scrutiny. He had a hearing aid in his right ear. Other than that, he appeared to be a healthy, seventy-some year-old man. "Tina says that you're related to Cassie. She's a sweet girl. I've met her a couple of times over the summer when Jerry brought her in for a piece of Sylvia's homemade pie. The best pies on this side of the mountain, if you ask me. You say you're her brother? I can see the resemblance."

Technically, Orwin and Cassandra looked nothing alike. Well, if you discounted the black hair and brown eyes. I could have said that Cassandra was my sister due to the same hair color, but the older brother routine resembled reality since Cassie's true older brother was still residing within distance of their coven. Hal seemed to have bought the cover story hook, line, and sinker.

"I hope the family emergency isn't something serious," Hal said, focusing on Orwin's reaction. "Cassie did mention that her aunt was sick, now that I think of it."

It appeared that the older gentleman wanted to run

us through one more test, but this was an easy one to pass. We'd been trying to seek out Cassandra for quite a while now. A couple of my premonitions had sidetracked us along the way, but Orwin had been able to put together quite the dossier on the young medium.

So, how was it possible that we'd miss someone by the name of Jerry?

If he was Cassandra's boyfriend, then the dramatic tale we'd conjured about her seeking shelter from any danger that might be prevalent held no weight. She would simply be a college girl who'd skipped a few days of school to be with the man she loved. If that was the case, then where would vampires fit into all of this?

"Our uncle is actually the one who hasn't been doing well," Orwin corrected Hal with a sad smile. He pushed up his glasses with his index finger. "I tried to call Cassie, but I couldn't get any calls through to her cell phone."

I hadn't noticed it before, but there had been a slight stiffness in Hal's shoulders. It dissipated gradually until Hal nodded his approval.

"I remember now," Hal responded with a small smile, which had more to do with his approval than it did with his memory. He had carried with him around the corner a stack of envelopes, which he now waved to the older couple enjoying their breakfast. He still carried on a conversation with us. "His heart?"

"That's right," Orwin responded, shifting his stance so that he could take a step closer to Hal. I realized that the six foot gap he needed to be within distance from someone to read their thoughts was just out of reach. "Is there a way for me to get a message to Cassie?"

"Not all the way up there at the fishing cabin." Hal began to make his way over to the older couple, unknowingly putting more distance between him and Orwin. "I'm sure they'll be stopping in for the package Jerry has been eagerly waiting on, so you'll want to settle in for a bit. Food is good, and the pie is even better. Never too early nor too late for a good piece of pie. That's my take on it."

It was moments like this that I missed having Pearl by our sides. She'd be able to convey what Orwin was thinking, giving me the ability to make a decision. The underlying energy in the diner seemed a bit…edgy. There was no other way to describe it.

We had a choice to make. Either we stayed and enjoyed breakfast while hoping that Jerry and Cassandra made an entrance, or we actively sought them out. The nudge I received in the arm by Orwin conveyed his choice loud and clear. There wasn't a remote chance I was getting him to leave the safety net he considered to be this diner anytime soon.

We were about to have ourselves a delicious piece of mystery pie.

Chapter Six

I'D GOTTEN IN the habit of watching my surroundings ever since my encounter with Ammeline Letty Romilda, much like I imagined a soldier who was in combat watched his surroundings. Knox called it situational awareness. I just thought of it as covering my rear end.

The older couple had thanked Hal for their mail, not bothering to hide their interest in the ongoing conversation. It was also the reason I'd noticed that only one person didn't seem to be intent on hearing the latest gossip, and that happened to be the young woman reading her book in one of the back booths.

"We'll do that," Orwin said, not taking Hal up on his offer quite yet. "We have another friend who was checking the other parts of town, hoping to spot Cassie. We'll go outside and flag her down."

We'd unhooked my red Jeep from the back of the RV after parking it at the campground. Piper had Pearl with her, so I wasn't too worried when they opted to drive up and down the main thoroughfare of this practically deserted small town. The cold weather didn't help things, but Cassandra Opal Saruman had come to hide in these mountains.

At least, that's what we'd thought in the beginning.

Now that we'd been given some answers, this might simply be a case of two college students in love taking time for themselves to enjoy a tryst. Why then had I foreseen Orwin's death? I'd almost had myself convinced that either Cassandra had sought help from a nest of vampires or they'd kidnapped her for her witchcraft abilities, but Jerry sounded like he was a prominent member of this town. What were we missing?

"We'll be back for that piece of pie," I said with a wave, taking Orwin's cue that he wanted to speak with me outside and away from prying eyes and ears. He hadn't been close enough to Hal or the other patrons to pick up what they may have been thinking, so I'm assuming an interesting thought had crossed Tina's mind. "Thanks for letting us know about Cassandra being up at the cabin."

Orwin and I quickly stepped outside, bracing ourselves against the bitter cold. It was an impossible feat, but we didn't have to worry about anyone overhearing us between the piercing gusts of winds and the rumble of the snowplow clearing the main street through town once again. My red Jeep was easy to spot coming toward us from the east.

"Tina gave Jerry a heads-up that we're looking for

Cassandra, but not for the reasons we would assume."
Orwin lifted a hand when Piper could finally see us. She
turned into the parking lot, claiming one of the many
open spots that lined the side of the building, bypassing
the two fuel pumps that were located between the front
door and the street. "Tina has no idea that there is a nest
of vampires living in these mountains. She just thought
Cassandra should know that her brother is in town."

It was a good thing that Cassandra did have a brother, but we had no idea if the sibling had any idea about
Jerry and West Virginia. If she hadn't ditched class and
come here for love, then she would now know that
someone had picked up her trail. That would have made
sense had Jerry been a vampire, but it was sounding more
and more as if he was human.

"Researching information online can definitely have
its disadvantages," Orwin explained before blowing his
warm breath into the palms of his hands. "Cassandra
never mentioned Jerry online. Not once. What we have
discovered by being here is that Tina knew Jerry from
high school, he flunked out of college, fell in love with
Cassandra, and they're most likely heading into town
this afternoon. I, for one, wouldn't mind staying in a
public place until this evening."

"What if Jerry is a warlock who has been camouflag-
ing this area for a nest of vampires?" I put the question
out there, because Orwin was right about us being at a
disadvantage. "We have no idea who or what we're

dealing with, other than Cassandra being a medium."

"I should stay here at the diner," Orwin proposed, his brows disappearing behind his glasses as he frowned. "Gas station or supply post, whatever this place is actually called."

I completely understood why Orwin would want to stay inside the diner portion of the building until the timeframe passed on my premonition, but I was hoping we'd locate the vampire who thought it was acceptable to drain the life out of a warlock without there being any repercussions. Breaking the unwritten peace treaty between vampires and witches wasn't the brightest idea, especially when said warlock had powerful allies.

"You realize that Jerry and Cassandra aren't going to come into town, right?" I had wrapped my burgundy scarf around my neck in a manner that allowed me to tuck the edges into my jacket, but that didn't stop the bitter cold from weaving its way through the fabric. The brutal winter weather wasn't the only thing leaving me cold. "We're going to have to go to them, which means finding the location of Jerry's residence when he's in town."

We're one step ahead of you, dear hexed one. You see, Jerry and Cassandra are already in town. My sweet Piper was wise enough to bring the map from the RV, along with the amethyst she used during her locator spell.

Pearl had joined us, leaving Piper to shut off the Jeep's engine. She grabbed her crossbody purse and slung it over her winter jacket, that just so happened to be a burnt orange, similar to that of a pumpkin spiced candle. There was no way she'd be able to wear that coat out into the woods and not be spotted from a mile away.

"Cassandra is close by?" Orwin asked, the hope lacing his tone hitting me squarely in the chest. In all the months of being hexed, I'd never once feared for my life. Maybe my sanity, but never my life. "Lou, stop with the guilt trip."

One would think that I'd never forget Orwin's ability to read minds within a six foot distance, but it was harder to control my thoughts than I was willing to admit.

"Sorry," I muttered, blinking furiously when my eyes began to water from another gust of wind. "Pearl, how close are Cassandra and this Jerry person?"

Miss Lilura, you will be pleased to know that we might not have to go anywhere near that wretched cabin. Miss Saruman and her beau happen to be parked around the other side of the building, and they are using the back entrance to retrieve a package as we speak.

By this time, Piper had joined us and continued to let Pearl explain that we should split up, though she would accompany Orwin back inside so there wasn't a chance he could be snatched out of the parking lot.

"It's not like I'm foolish enough to take candy out of a stranger's hand and hop into a white van," Orwin protested, shoving his fists back inside his coat pockets.

Should the kidnapper be a little green man with a map

of the universe, I have no doubt that you'd take your chances, alien hunter. I hope that you've taken your allergy medicine this morning, because I'll be by your side the rest of the day.

I could hear Pearl mention how she'd love to enjoy a spot of warm cream during breakfast as she walked away with Orwin, doing her best to keep his mind off the premonition. She was doing a good job of it, too.

"Let's go," I said to Piper, not wanting to waste any more time. It would have really helped to have Knox in on this endeavor, though I wasn't worried we couldn't handle this confrontation on our own. "First things first. We make sure that Cassandra knows we're not here to hurt her, and also mention that we know about the vampire's nest. If she doesn't, then we'll improvise. That should at least get her talking to us, giving us a chance to change the outcome of my vision."

Piper's blue eyes deepened with worry as we both broke into a light jog, mindful of the icy areas in the parking lot. Neither one of us said anything else until we'd made it around the corner, finally catching sight of a young man who must be Jerry speaking with Hal in the open doorway.

Whether or not Jerry was a human, vampire, or a warlock, I was betting on him knowing about Cassandra's bloodline. I would work out something to say to the older gentleman after we'd had a private conversation with Cassandra. In the meantime, I did the only thing I could that would guarantee things would work in our favor.

With the residual energy that I was always harnessing from the earth, I expended the momentum and all but shoved Jerry into the older gentleman as gently as I could and slammed the door shut behind them. Cassandra had been a few feet away, huddled in a long black dress coat that probably cost more than my entire outfit. She'd been born into one of the wealthier covens, which could be the reason she'd kept Jerry hidden from her family thus far.

Should Jerry turn out to be a vampire, that type of union would never have been allowed into the fold due to the danger of the coven being exposed to the world. Same with a human, which gave credence to Jerry being a warlock and possibly the one cloaking this entire mountain for the undead to have a place to rest.

"How are we going to explain your little shove to the people inside? A gust of wind?" Piper asked in disbelief, holding up her hands to Cassandra to indicate that we weren't a threat. That was kind of hard to do after the brute force I just utilized, but it had been necessary. "Cassandra, we just want to talk! I promise that we're not here to hurt you or Jerry."

It was easy to see that Cassandra was torn; she didn't have the same abilities as me to protect herself—what she had was even stronger than telekinesis. It was evident from her hesitation that she'd yet to come into her full powers. Did she not know that even a sliver of her ancestors' powers could hurt us in unspeakable ways?

"Cassandra, we're in trouble," I said hastily, having already distinguished that she was exactly like Piper. She wouldn't be here helping Jerry otherwise, which proved that she had a heart of gold. It didn't matter if she was here as a friend, lover, or just to lend a helping hand. The situation might very well be reversed, and she'd either sought out Jerry's help or the other way around. Either way, her heart was in the right place. "Please give us five minutes to talk to you."

I wasn't beyond begging to make sure that Orwin lived to see another day. Piper and I had slowly been walking toward Cassandra, not wanting her to make a run for the vehicle. We had no idea if the keys were inside, and neither one of us wanted to be run over with a car.

"Please, Cassandra. It's a matter of—"

A horrible, muffled scream came from behind the door which I'd all but shoved Jerry through in my attempt to have a moment alone with the young medium. Something terrifying must be happening inside…the one place where Orwin and Pearl had sought safety.

Chapter Seven

"ORWIN!" I CALLED out, having been the first through the thick greyish door. Piper and Cassandra were close on the heels of my winter boots, but Jerry and Hal were nowhere in sight in the room that must serve as a mail storage facility. I didn't waste time and made my way quickly into the small dining area. "Orwin!"

I kept expecting him to answer, but all I could make out were the frightened screams of the other patrons. The high-pitched panic had been coming from Tina, who was cowering behind the counter of the cash register. An older gentleman was trying to calm his wife, who was practically barreling her way out through the front glass door. The woman who'd been enjoying her coffee was lying flat in the booth with her hands over her head in protection, while Orwin appeared unharmed and crouched over the man who'd been enjoying his breakfast earlier.

"Piper, I need your help," Orwin called out from a kneeling position on the hardwood floor. "He was hit in the head, but he's still breathing."

That wasn't simply a hit to the head, Mr. Cornelia. Miss Saruman's beau certainly had an arm on him, didn't he? Nice of you to join us, dear hexed one.

"What happened, Orwin?" I asked, hoping that Pearl would take my hint and keep talking. Tina had finally composed herself and was already frantically speaking into the phone, most likely with whatever police presence this small town utilized as law enforcement. Cassandra had skidded to a stop in order to hear what Tina had to say, although she kept a wary gaze on all of us as Piper tended to the victim. "Please tell me that Jerry…"

Miss Saruman's wariness is due to her detecting my presence. She can hear my thoughts. In turn, I can hear hers. The two of you might want to take a look at the bag next to the table. It explains quite a bit, although I do see our medium deciding if she's going to make a run for the door.

My gaze dropped to the black duffel bag that had been stored underneath the table where the unconscious man had been eating his breakfast. Sure enough, a wooden handle stuck out of the bag. The crossbow certainly began to clear up a lot of the mystery that had surrounded this mountaintop. Unfortunately, I couldn't take time to inspect the weapon without taking a chance that Cassandra would utilize my distraction to her advantage and make good on her getaway.

My sweet Piper's latest patient does indeed appear to be a vampire hunter, dear hexed one. We now know the reason for the concealing incantation. It appears as if Miss

Saruman disguised her friend's home in order to protect him from an agonizing death. Am I right, Miss Saruman?

So, Jerry was a vampire, and Cassandra was the witch helping him stay under the radar. A part of me was relieved that we had nothing to do with the medium's need to flee her life at the college, but we were still somehow connected to her due to my premonition.

"Sheriff Tate is on her way over, and she's asking for everyone to stay put until she arrives," Tina called out with a shaky voice. By this time, I had already made my way over to the front of the dining area to make sure that Cassandra didn't sneak out after Jerry through the front door. I also wanted to be close enough to speak to her without anyone else overhearing, but Tina didn't seem inclined to leave the counter. She was quite content to allow someone else to attend to the man lying on the floor. "Cassie, why would Jerry attack that guy? Did they know each other?"

Miss Saruman is very young, dear hexed one. I do not believe she harnesses enough power to get through you to the exit.

The fact that Tina didn't know the stranger who had been eating breakfast gave more credence that the man was a vampire hunter. I guess we had our answer as to whether or not Jerry was a human, a warlock, or a bloodsucking creature who just happened to have a very good throwing arm. Seeing a small one-pound weight from the scale that Hal probably kept in the mail room on the floor next to the unconscious man, it didn't take a genius to figure out what weapon had been utilized in what was looking more and more like self-defense.

We mean you no harm, Miss Saruman. Perhaps we might even be able to help you with your current predicament involving the hunter lying on the floor? His name is Mr. Palisade.

While Cassandra and Pearl were having a conversation that would hopefully reassure Cassandra that we meant no harm, I still wasn't so sure her concern over Jerry wouldn't have her sneaking out the exit. I strategically positioned myself between her and the front door, thus giving me full view of the sheriff quickly walking across the street. The older couple made their way outside, not heeding Tina's request that they remain inside the building.

The short-order cook and another waitress, the only other two employees the diner seemed to have on staff this morning, were near the small kitchen. They were whispering to one another in hushed tones. As for the woman in the booth, she'd cautiously sat in an upright position to see what damage had been done to the other patron.

"I don't think Jerry knew the man," Cassandra responded softly, her gaze leaving me to glance at the front door. She'd lost a bit of color in her face when she saw that the sheriff was about to enter the diner. Sheriff Tate had already dismissed the older couple. "I'm not sure why Jerry would hurt a stranger, unless he had felt threatened by him. Did they have much of a heated exchange, Tina?"

Before Tina could reply, Mr. Palisade let out a guttural groan as Piper helped him into a seated position. He held the balled-up napkins against the open cut on the side of his head. She was asking him for details on what had happened, but he didn't seem to be very forthcoming.

I would agree with you on the self-defense claim, Miss Lilura, although this vampire hunter does seem to be a bit careless with his weapons. Mr. Palisade could be new to the fold, of course. On another note, Miss Saruman's love interest clearly doesn't want the locals knowing the true nature of his undead state, otherwise he would have done what is instinctive to his kind. Isn't that right, Miss Saruman?

"I was talking to Mr. and Mrs. Hickman about the weather. I didn't see anything, other than to catch Jerry and Hal running for the front door. As for Mr. Palisade, he was driving through town when the storm hit last night," Tina managed to say about the hunter who was only now coming to after Piper had discreetly used her ability to ensure the sheriff wasn't about to walk in on a murder scene. Cassandra must have replied to Pearl by thought, leaving me to guess that the reply had been affirmative to Pearl's theory. "Maggie gave him a place to stay above the bar last night. Cassie, do you know Mr. Palisade?"

"No." Cassandra was staring at me with hesitation

and concern, most likely trying to figure out exactly who we were and why we'd been looking for her. Pearl had only been able to convey that we meant her no harm. While whatever concealing spell this medium had used around the nest had been good enough to hide Jerry's residence, she hadn't thought or had enough power to do the same with the town. "Where did Jerry go, Tina? I should really find out what happened and try to convince him to speak with the sheriff."

Miss Saruman has agreed to hear us out, but only if we come up with a cover for her friend.

"Jerry and Hal ran out the front after Jerry completely lost his mind. I mean, he just lost it." Tina's cheeks were regaining a bit of their color, and she sighed with relief when the front door finally opened to reveal a woman with short blonde hair. She was wearing a grey sheriff's uniform with a matching coat, and she certainly didn't look happy that she'd been called away from the warmth of her office. "Sheriff, I'm so glad you're here. Jerry took off, but he was the one who threw that scale weight at Mr. Palisade."

"Is Jerry up to his old tricks again?" Sheriff Tate asked in a knowing tone that indicated she'd had a few run-ins with Jerry before. She surveyed those who remained in the building, probably taking in the fact that the majority were out-of-towners. "Let me guess. Hal got him out of the building before you called me."

It appears that Hal and Miss Saruman's beau have a

special connection. There seems to be a lot of secrets in this town, does there not?

The sheriff flicked her narrowed gaze from Tina to me, then from Cassandra to where Piper and Orwin were helping the man back into his chair at the table. She clearly didn't like the fact that there were so many strangers involved in a local incident.

"Cassie, didn't you learn your lesson the last time you visited Jerry? Tell me. Is he back on drugs? Don't answer that just yet. I'll get your statement after speaking with the victim," Sheriff Tate directed before indicating that she wanted Cassandra to take a seat on the bench next to the front door. "Who are you, ma'am?"

It looks as if you have a decision to make, Miss Lilura. Do we help cover for a vampire or do we somehow finagle our way out of this situation and move on?

Chapter Eight

"Lou," I ANSWERED, feeling the weight of Cassandra's stare. I didn't bother to give my last name. I was hoping that it wouldn't come to that, given that we were in vampire territory. While the UV rays of the sun bothered creatures of the night, the shadowed, grey filtered sunlight of a day like today didn't prevent them from moving about during the daytime. Given the time of year, the usual coverage of winter clothing and overcast skies, there was nothing to stop them from enjoying the outdoors. "I'm here with Cassie's brother. We couldn't reach her on her cell phone to let her know that her uncle is in the hospital."

"I'm sorry to hear that, Cassie. I'll let you get on your way shortly. Why don't the two of you grab a seat for now?"

Sheriff Tate waited until Cassandra and I had done as she asked, settling ourselves onto the rickety old bench. Surprisingly enough, it held our weight. We sat in silence as we watched the sheriff walk over to where Mr. Palisade was listening quite intently to whatever Orwin and Piper were saying to him.

Our alien hunter seems to be a bit out of sorts today. I'm assuming it's due to your premonition about his impending death, but it does seem to give him an assertiveness that is much needed in this situation. You'll be happy to know that Mr. Cornelia has taken care of things on his end, and Mr. Palisade will do as we've asked of him.

"You're the ones who wanted to meet with me back in Minnesota," Cassandra whispered, guessing correctly. She also noticed that Tina had finally moved from behind the counter so that she could listen in on the sheriff's conversation with Mr. Palisade. "I'm sorry that I skipped out, but Jerry needed my help."

"Is he the reason you haven't visited your coven in the last six months?" I asked, guessing at some of the missing puzzle pieces that had Pearl's intuition all but screaming that something was wrong with the scenario. "Your family has no idea that you're dating a vampire, do they?"

My intuition doesn't scream, dear hexed one. That would be uncharacteristically rude. In case you are wondering what is being said, Mr. Palisade is explaining that he provoked Miss Saruman's beau into throwing a one-pound scale weight at his head. I realize how the story sounds, and so does the rather apathetic sheriff. I do believe that she'd rather wash her hands of this dispute than write it all up, and she is willing to believe the absurd tale despite her skepticism.

"Jerry and I love one another," Cassandra defended,

clutching her hands in her lap. She was wearing black leather gloves, and it didn't appear that she was going to take them off. That was one indication that she didn't believe she'd be inside this building for very much longer. "He called me…scared and terrified that he was being hunted by someone new. He asked for my help, and I couldn't say no. Tell me what it is you want. I'll do it, but only if you promise to help me keep Jerry and his family safe."

You should know from your childhood lessons that one bite from a vampire could cost you your life, Miss Saruman. We do not take that lightly, and it is the sole reason we keep our distance.

"Not the sole reason," I amended wryly, indicating that we also didn't prefer how vampires got their source of nutrition if they happened to go on a bender. "You have yourself a deal, Cassandra, but only if you can get Jerry to guarantee our safety."

My first concern was Orwin and ensuring that my premonition was altered to the point that it never happened in reality. Nothing else mattered at this moment…even my hex.

And you wonder why I'm so fond of you, Miss Lilura.

"Don't start, Pearl," I said, keeping my focus on Cassandra. "Do we have a deal? You get Jerry to tell all of his bloodsucking friends that we're completely off limits. If they break that truce, I'll have every coven from this coast to the next informed that the treaty has been broken by your friend's nest."

Now who's showing her assertiveness? I'm once again impressed with your dedication to your traveling band of merry misfits.

"Jerry nor his family would ever hurt anyone, let alone a witch," Cassandra whispered back, the faith she had in Jerry evident in her plea. "You make it sound as if there are hundreds of vampires on this mountain. There aren't. Jerry is the only vampire within thirty miles from this town, and he's a good man. I promise you that no one will get hurt. Please help me."

If I may offer my opinion, Miss Lilura, she does sound sincere.

"Alright, folks," Sheriff Tate called out, though there was only one true customer still at her booth. "Let's call it a morning and go about your business."

"Is there anything we need to know, Pearl?" I straightened when Sheriff Tate began to walk our way, stopping briefly to ask Tina about her version of events. "Did anyone contradict Mr. Palisade?"

Mr. Palisade refused medical treatment, though he has no idea that my sweet Piper healed the concussion he suffered at the hands of Miss Saruman's beau. The chef— and I use that term loosely—was with the other waitress in the back kitchen when the confrontation ensued, and Tina was speaking with the older couple. The young woman in the booth had her nose in a book, and she didn't notice a thing. You might want to ask Miss Saruman about the postmaster, though. Let's just say that he wasn't forced to leave with her beau, but instead seemed to be leading the way.

Pearl had finished a recount of the last few moments, and just in the nick of time.

"Cassie, I'm sorry to hear that your uncle is in such poor health," Sheriff Tate said, beginning to put back on her grey knit gloves. "Jerry doesn't get a pass, though. Just because Mr. Palisade started the argument, that doesn't give Jerry the right to assault the man or to leave the way he did. Jerry is very fortunate that Mr. Palisade isn't pressing charges, but I'll still need to speak with him regardless."

It appears that Sheriff Tate is not aware that a vampire runs amuck in her small town, as is the same story with the other locals. Miss Saruman, just how long has your beau been one of the undead?

"We just got back from the fishing cabin, but I'm meeting him at Hal's place," Cassandra replied as smooth as any experienced witch. She'd been taught well, and her abilities would grow in time. Her limited skill did give me pause in my belief that she could reach out to the ancestors who had knowledge on how to break a curse as strong as one bestowed by a Lich Queen. "Jerry was just acting in self-defense. He was scared that you wouldn't see it his way, given his past troubles. He's still struggling with the whole college debacle that happened last year."

Miss Saruman is trying to tell us that her beau was newly initiated to the vampire lifestyle. No wonder he had such trouble controlling his more violent impulses. That might explain why the alien hunter became such a delicious snack in your premonition, dear hexed one.

"I take it you were hoping to leave for Minnesota today?" Sheriff Tate asked Cassandra, though the woman was staring at me. She might not know that vampires lived on the outskirts of her town, but she was aware that all was not right with Jerry and Cassandra. "You'll want to rethink your trip. Another storm is blowing down from the northwest. It'll make this one look like a light dusting in comparison. Maggie should have another room or two above the bar. I'll touch base with her and tell her she'll be having more guests this evening."

"Thank you, Sheriff," Cassandra murmured, answering for us without even blinking. She quickly stood from the rickety bench, which somehow still supported my weight. "I'll let Jerry know you're stopping by to speak with him, and I'll also make sure he remains at his uncle's place until you arrive."

Miss Saruman seems quite confident we are willing to stay overnight within hunting distance of a vampire. I'm not so sure that is the wisest of choices, dear hexed one. The short amount of time that Mr. Cornelia and I have spent together has been, shall we say, quite difficult on my well-preserved patience. May I suggest we take care of our needs and be on our way before he begins crafting me an aluminum foil hat?

I stood and made sure to shake hands with the sheriff, who was only doing her duty in ensuring that the situation had turned out for the best. Had she known the real story, this situation could have taken a turn for the worse.

As for Cassandra, she was probably questioning our sanity with talk of aliens, aluminum foil hats, and hexes. It was best we have more privacy to discuss the important details on what needed to happen next, plus I wasn't leaving this medium's side until I spoke to Jerry. Someone had turned him, and not by coincidence, that someone belonged to a nest of these creatures. A truce needed to be negotiated with the leader, and then we could get down to business.

"I'll ride with you, Cassandra," I said, ensuring that my statement wasn't taken as a suggestion. We technically weren't going anywhere until we all had a chat with Mr. Palisade. His name wasn't all that original, but we needed to convince him to leave this particular subject alone. "Your brother and Piper can follow in the Jeep."

Well done, dear hexed one. While garlic only slows undead critters down, I'll use the drive to rub some on my fur. It might very well clear out Mr. Cornelia's sinuses. Oh, the things we shall accomplish today!

Chapter Nine

"WE DON'T HAVE time for this," Cassandra replied with irritation as I all but forced her to take a seat at the table with Mr. Palisade. She was shooting daggers his way with a simple glare, so I made sure that she sat across from him. "And I don't want to be anywhere near this murderer."

It's not nice to irritate the man who has come here to eradicate the vampire inhabiting this mountain, Miss Saruman. May I suggest a spot of warm cream? It does wonders for one's disposition.

"Not now, Pearl," I muttered, pulling up another chair so that we could all make some small talk before taking that drive deeper into the mountains. Hopefully, Knox had been able to check out those locations on the map and make it back in time to fill us in on which cabin was the site in which I'd seen Orwin's impending death take place. Knox was going on description only, but it would have to do for now. "Mr. Palisade, we need to come to some sort of arrangement that has you leaving this mountain before the next storm front rolls in. What

THE CURSE THAT BITES   67

we do here could very well save your life."

"Monster?" Frank Palisade practically hissed in disgust, ignoring my request. He was still holding some napkins against the side of his head to blot the wound that had miraculously dissipated. Piper had healed the internal damage, but she'd refrained from closing the laceration completely in fear of someone noticing her magic. She'd played it safe, but I wasn't so sure we should let the smaller injury heal itself when a vampire could smell fresh blood from a very long distance. "You're the monsters, sucking the blood out of us humans as if we're nothing more than an all-you-can-eat buffet."

Mr. Palisade does have a point, though it's apparent that he has confused Miss Saruman for one of the undead creatures he seeks. Maybe it would be best to enlighten him before he attempts to take her life and truly regrets such an action.

"Mr. Palisade, she is not a vampire," I whispered, quickly scooting my chair closer to the table. Orwin shook his head at me to indicate nothing I had to say about the situation was going to change Frank's opinion of vampires. "What do you know of the supernatural? You seem a bit confused."

Mr. Cornelia would like you to know that Miss Saruman managed to steal the red pepper off the table. I can only assume that she has memorized the incantation that will bring Mr. Palisade under her control. She might be relatively new in the spell department, but I do so admire her determination.

Red pepper was known for its ability to influence someone's thoughts and perceptions. Utilized with the right spell, Mr. Palisade could actually be forced to forget this moment and move on with his life.

I was really big on choice, though.

"What I know is that these creatures need to be eradicated from this planet before we all end up dead. She might not be one of them, but she's been protecting that fiend living up there in those mountains." Frank leaned back just in time as the waitress approached us cautiously. She wasn't too happy that we were still here, and I wondered if she'd gone to school with Jerry, as well. "I'd like my bill, please. I'm leaving."

Piper gave the waitress the brightest smile as she stopped in front of us.

"Would it be possible to get a box of those mini-blueberry muffins and a couple of those fruit pies to go? Cherry and apple, if you have them. Mr. Palisade is being kind enough to pay everyone's tab who was here this morning when he mistakenly provoked Jerry." Piper tilted her head just so, causing a blonde curl to escape its messy bun. "Isn't that right, Mr. Palisade?"

I do love when my lessons pay off. My sweet Piper can tango with the best of them.

Frank tossed the sullied napkins down next to his plate, clearly not liking how the tables had been turned. The only benefit to this situation was that we were aware of the hunters' rules of engagement, and one of them clearly stated that those humans who remained in the dark regarding vampires shall remain so in order not to create panic.

I'd love to see the reaction of these vampire hunters should they learn of all the other supernatural creatures in existence. They wouldn't be so pompous with their crossbows and oak bolts, now would they?

Try to rein yourself in, dear hexed one. We all know that karma has the last say in situations like these.

"Of course," the waitress said in agreement, most likely willing to do whatever it took to get all of us out the door. "Cassie, would you like something extra to take to Jerry?"

"That would be great, Julie," Cassandra replied, attempting to cover up her agitation that I'd been able to take away the red pepper shaker from her hands underneath the table.

The waitress didn't show it, but she had caught onto Piper's scheme. Julie happily went along with it. Ten percent of a larger ticket meant a bigger tip. The fact that she and Cassandra had such a friendly rapport told me that maybe our medium had been dating Jerry longer than the six months we'd previously surmised.

No, my dear hexed. The two lovebirds met in early summer quite by accident, and the two have basically been inseparable since.

"I'm not letting this bounty get away, so you can just save your breath." Frank leaned down and reached for his bag, frowning even more, if that were possible. He angrily shoved the part of his bow that had been exposed back into his bag. "I get why you would mess with my gear, but what I don't understand is why you would tip your hand to these monsters. They'll betray you and drain your blood."

Orwin and I exchanged confused glances. Bounty? Normally, vampire hunters didn't work on that type of system. They traveled across the globe in search of unexplained deaths that would lead them to the undead they reviled. There wasn't an organization who oversaw the minions, nor was there a system of barter in place, per se.

Unless Miss Saruman's beau did the unspeakable to a family member of some hunters, it is very rare such a bounty would be placed on the head of a specific undead creature.

"We didn't mess with anything of yours," Orwin said, clearing up the first misunderstanding. As for the second, I wasn't so sure that Frank would be willing to share those details. Hunters were known for their privacy, because that's how they survived. "Who has the bounty on their head? Is it for Jerry or someone associated with him?"

Miss Saruman's beau might have restrained his instinct to protect his friends and family, but beware that she has no qualms of protecting him at great lengths.

Cassandra refused to meet my gaze, which confirmed Pearl's suspicion that the young medium would utilize magic in front of those remaining in this diner. It had somehow become our responsibility to make sure that didn't happen, while at the same time ensuring Orwin's safety.

Frank remained silent, realizing that he'd made a mistake about revealing the existence of a bounty. It didn't matter that he refused to respond to any more questions. Orwin had already read his thoughts and received the answers we sought. We just needed to ask the right questions and siphon off the right information.

Our resident warlock is also the only one who can figure out what particular carrot or stick it would take to have Mr. Palisade leaving this mountain posthaste. Let's see what you come up with, alien hunter. Shall we place a wager? If you accomplish your mission on the first go round, I'll tell you something about those little green men and the pyramids back in my dear Cleopatra days. Should you fail, you'll not speak of any unidentified flying objects for one week.

Okay, then.

Clearly, Pearl and Orwin had spent way too much time together in the last fifteen or sixteen hours that had now passed since my premonition. Even though we'd all been inside the RV, Pearl had made it her personal mission to stay glued to Orwin's side every minute. The only break the two had been given was those few short moments that he'd entered the diner with me.

All is fair in allergies and conspiracy theories, dear hexed one.

A group of four older gentleman came walking through the front door, greeting Tina in a way that told us they were regulars. It wasn't a surprise when one of them brought up Jerry. The fact that Frank Palisade was still sitting at our table with strangers arriving wasn't in our favor.

"Mr. Palisade, why do you think Jerry Kline risked coming into town today?"

Risked? Hadn't Jerry and Cassandra ventured into town due to the package? Orwin had picked up something useful in Frank Palisade's thoughts, though it might very well have been Cassandra's mind. If the package had been shipped from Minnesota, that would mean it came from someone close to Cassandra. Maybe material items to conduct some type of incantation that would provide Jerry with a safety net.

"I'm not answering any more of your questions," Frank said with determination, hoisting the black bag over his shoulder. "I don't know who you people are, but Jerry Kline is my prize to turn over. I'll be the one collecting that cash reward."

"Now will you give me back that red pepper?" Cassandra murmured in clear desperation.

Patience, Miss Saruman.

"Jerry sensed you from miles away, and what he now has in his possession is a list of names of everyone who took that bounty," Orwin shared, his tone so unlike the easy-going conspiracy theorist who we were used to in our everyday lives.

Well, that was innovative. The package that Jerry took

with him upon leaving this building was material compo-
nents for a more complete incantation that Cassandra would
like to cast in order to protect him. Well done, Mr.
Cornelia. I shall reserve my congratulations until Mr.
Palisade departs this mountain.

The more time that passed by in the twenty-four-
hour timeframe of my premonition, the further Orwin
was willing to go to make sure that it wasn't him that
met a fateful end. He was willing to do or say just about
anything to save this man's life. It was well-known that
for vampires to remain among the supernatural from
their earlier years of inception, they had to adapt their
rules. Number one? No taking a human life unless you
were willing to suffer the consequences of your actions. I
wasn't privy to the entirety of their code, but Orwin was
improvising to buy us more time to figure out this new
mystery and what it was all about.

"I don't believe you," Frank scoffed, though the fact
he leaned back in his chair and didn't attempt to leave
the diner said otherwise. He shook his head in increduli-
ty, letting his bag drop to the floor with a thud. He met
each of our stares as he sorted through the thoughts in
his head, unaware that Orwin was listening to each and
every one. "There's no way to find out that information
unless you're a member of the brotherhood."

"No?" Orwin asked, somehow seeming even more
confident than before.

There's a reason for that, dear hexed one. Mr. Cornelia's
ability to read the human mind certainly comes in handy

during these types of investigations. It's looking more and more as if I might have to fork over what I know of the hieroglyphics inside the pyramid regarding those little green men our alien hunter has become so obsessed with over the years. I should warn you now that a trip to Nevada might be in our near future, Miss Lilura.

"You received the bounty information through an online app where messages are exchanged. Did you or did you not reply with the code word *caterpillar?*"

"Yes," Frank answered, leaning forward so that the four men who'd taken a table couldn't quite make out what we were discussing. "What does that have to do with anything?"

"It means that all it takes is a decent hacker to retrieve the names of those who responded through linked IP addresses," Orwin explained, not giving Frank time to ask any more questions. "We were hired to clean up this mess, which means you are leaving this mountain…now. Go home. No more hunting until you're given the all clear codeword—*grapevine.*"

I'm rather impressed, alien hunter.

I wasn't just impressed. I was proud, too. Orwin had figured out a way to not only give us leeway to speak with Cassandra and Jerry in private, but he'd also guaranteed this man's safety. There was no telling what Jerry would do to a hunter who'd put innocent lives at risk by his carelessness when it came to failing to conceal his weapons in public.

Frank had bought the cover story, and his imagination had even added credence to Orwin's fabrication of the facts, all because he was aware of the proper code words.

"You're probably here to get the list of names before he can distribute them," Frank guessed, looking at Cassandra with admiration. He leaned back against his chair with a creepy smile on his face. I'm not so sure that his enjoyment was only ridding the planet of the undead; so much so that he was worse than a vampire nest, which at least followed a moral code. I was now regretting taking those red pepper flakes from Cassandra. "I get it now. Fine. I'll leave, but I expect to be contacted as soon as this situation is resolved. I got word of a rather nasty nest in Maine."

"There will be a notice in the app when the job is complete. Look for the codeword you've been given." Orwin tapped the table in a final act of authority. Unfortunately, he sneezed…three times. Any sense of influence went right out the window, though he did his best to recover. "I suggest you leave now while there's still time before the storm hits, and before we have to extract you ourselves."

It seems as if Mr. Cornelia is in need of a tissue.

"Pay up," Orwin muttered behind the napkin that Piper had slid over to him. Frank was already standing, holding out his hand for the check. Julie relinquished the bill over after she set the two to-go bags down on the table. "Thank you, Julie."

"You're welcome, sweetie pie," Julie replied with a wink. "I included my tip to help you out."

I think my eyes are burning, Miss Lilura. What was that?

"Flirting," Orwin replied with a grin and a red nose after Julie had turned her attention to the four older men at the other table. His smile quickly faded when reality overshadowed his temporary lapse of judgement. "Which I might not survive to enjoy if we don't take care of our vampire problem."

"Do you really think the hunter is going to leave this mountain?" Cassandra asked, her worried gaze following the man out the door after he'd slapped some cash down on the counter in front of Tina. "Do you believe Jerry is safe now?"

"Unfortunately, that was only a temporary solution," I replied honestly, scooting my chair back and indicating that it was time to go. "We'll talk more in the car. Piper, you ride with Orwin. Follow close behind. Pearl and I will accompany Cassandra. It's time to get the entire story."

And maybe, dear hexed one, the answers we seek regarding your hex.

Chapter Ten

"WE HELPED YOU, Cassandra, as promised," I said, sliding the seat belt over my jacket. The beat-up old Chevy had seen better days. It was no wonder Jerry had trouble driving this thing in the winter. I just hoped that the incoming storm held off until tonight. "Now, I want the whole story as to how you got yourself involved with a vampire."

Young love knows no bounds, dear hexed one. Speaking of which, have we heard from our resident werewolf?

"Werewolf?" Cassandra had yet to pull the car out from behind the building, waiting for the engine to warm up a bit. Her head practically rotated like an owl as she searched for any sign of a lycanthrope. "I thought Orwin was a warlock."

That he is, among other things. Werewolf isn't one of them. You can also add an allergic conspiracy theorist to your list, though he does have good intentions.

"Orwin *is* a warlock." I motioned for her to drive, not wanting to waste any more time. She'd already assured me that we weren't going near a cabin. "Let's just say that we have our own more than capable reinforcements. We had no idea what we were going to encounter on this mountain."

"I already told you that Jerry is the only vampire within thirty miles. You won't need a pack of werewolves," Cassandra said in frustration, finally shifting the gear into drive while still wearing her black gloves. She maneuvered the car around the building until my red Jeep came into view. Piper was behind the wheel, having already backed out of the parking spot so that she could fall right in behind us as we turned onto the main road. "He doesn't want any trouble with anyone."

If that is the case, Miss Saruman, why is there an active bounty on your beau?

"I met Jerry at the beginning of summer during a college visit," Cassandra began as she kept the speed of the vehicle beneath the posted sign. The roads were still slick with packed icy snow in spots here and there. "We hit it off, but something horrible happened on his drive back from Minnesota to West Virginia. He didn't even have to call me. I just…felt it."

There are certain times that witches, such as Miss Saruman, can sense when they've met their true soulmate. It's rare, but it does happen from time to time. Her ancestors on the other side must have been keeping tabs on her beau. It would explain how she'd known something tragic had occurred to Mr. Kline.

"You can call me Cassie."

"Pearl has a thing about etiquette," I explained wryly,

not surprised to find that Pearl had made herself visible on my lap. Her sleek white fur was as bright as the ridges of snow that rested on the branches of the trees in the forest. "What happened on Jerry's drive back to West Virginia?"

Mr. Kline obviously met up with a vampire on the hunt, dear hexed one. Would you please turn the vent in a different direction? This vehicle reeks of the undead, and I'd rather not have to carry that particular rancid fragrance around on my fur. I mean no disrespect, Miss Saruman.

"Jerry was with his older brother, Paul." Cassandra frowned at the insult Pearl had unsuccessfully tried to soften. "They made a road trip out of the college visit, taking their time to see the sights on the way back home. Paul has a tendency to get into trouble without even looking, and he somehow got into an altercation that led to both him and Jerry being left for dead, buried in a shallow grave."

Vampires don't simply leave something of that significance to chance, Miss Saruman. With that said, the undead do tend to have heightened emotions when it comes to retaliation. Whatever altercation Mr. Paul Kline attracted clearly upset one of the vampires in question.

"Well, they didn't break the number one rule," I said, figuring the final outcome was better than the alternative. Pearl's green gaze landed on me in surprise, probably because I'd been trying to be a bit positive for a change. "I thought you said that Jerry was the only vampire within a thirty-mile distance. What happened to

Paul?"

"Paul up and left," Cassandra finally revealed, flipping on a turn signal. I didn't like the looks of the area. It sure resembled an out of the way setting that would contain a cabin, such as the one I was doing my best to keep Orwin away from until seven o'clock tonight. "He loved the power he'd gained in his transition, but he was afraid he'd hurt those he cared for by accident."

Wise decision, but why would your beau be different? He's still very new at vampirism, Miss Saruman.

"Let me guess," I said, looking over my shoulder to confirm that Piper was still on our tail. She was practically on our bumper. "Jerry called you, told you that he wasn't going to attend college, and you suspected something was wrong."

"Something like that. You see, we'd made plans to get together over the summer. One minute we were going to a water park the week after graduation, and the next he was saying he never wanted to see me again." Cassandra shrugged as she began to slow the car down, carefully managing to maneuver the tires over a gravel road that had been cleared by a snowplow. Probably a truck with one of those single lane plow blades on the front grill. "I don't know how to explain it, but I just knew that something was terribly wrong. I was still seventeen at the time, so I couldn't just get up and leave Minnesota. I waited until the day after my high school graduation, and then I talked a friend of mine into coming to West Virginia with me. Let's just say that she knows about what I am."

You realize that we have rules, too. It's not wise to tell our secrets to uninitiated humans, Miss Saruman.

I had a feeling that Cassandra wasn't one to follow the rules as much as she was to break them. It wasn't that she was a bad person—or witch. It had more to do with being isolated in a very large world and wanting more than anything to share her secrets with someone else for her own mental health.

Youth. There is a reason for wisdom, dear hexed one.

"Yeah, well, I can relate," I muttered, recalling the day I turned eighteen. It was if it was yesterday. I also understood what Pearl meant about wisdom, because I'd been so caught up with wanting to live my life that I'd abandoned the witchcraft that could very well be what saved my life in the very end. "Cassandra, we're not here to judge you. What happened when you and your friend finally made it here?"

"I found Uncle Hal first. He explained that something bad had happened to both of his nephews, but Paul had left the mountain almost immediately. They'd somehow managed to keep the rest of the family from finding out the truth, but Hal wasn't in the position to turn away my help. He is a human. I couldn't allow Jerry to hurt anyone, let alone an animal. Let's just say that I managed to convince one of the hospital staff on the other side of the mountain to give me a monthly supply of expired blood bags in exchange for some favors. They throw the expired blood out anyway. No one is going to miss it."

Oh, I could really do with a spot of warm cream. Did you catch all of that, dear hexed one? Our medium has been dishing out favors for bags of human blood. I believe I might have figured out the reason Miss Saruman's powers aren't as strong as they should be. And here I chalked it up to being young. Wishful thinking on my part.

It was a well-known fact that a medium's power was drawn from her ancestors, not necessarily from the earth. If Cassandra had upset those in the afterlife with her aiding and abetting a vampire, there would be consequences to face. Not to mention paying off a greedy human partner in crime.

Not only do we need to keep Mr. Cornelia alive until seven o'clock this evening, we are now in the company of a medium who has intentionally upset the balance of nature to serve her own purposes. Lest we forget the incoming blizzard that could very well keep all of us from leaving this mountain.

"I can hear the two of you," Cassandra exclaimed in displeasure, finally parking the car in front of a one-story house. I was able to release some of the tension that had built up in my shoulders at the thought that we were going to end up in front of a small log cabin. Cassandra didn't shut off the engine, though. She continued to explain the reason for the cloaking spell. "Over the summer, Jerry learned how to live his life as one of the undead without hunting prey."

Cassandra let her head fall back against the headrest, a smile of pride softening her lips. Her love for Jerry Kline was evident by the faraway look in her blue eyes, and it was in this moment that I truly comprehended the lengths she'd go to in order to guarantee his safety.

Yes, by infuriating a very long line of ancestors on the other side. Do you see why this might be a problem for us, dear hexed one?

"Tina mentioned that Jerry flunked out of college, which means that he at least began the first semester of his freshman year," I recalled, purposefully cutting off any questions Cassandra may have regarding Pearl's dire supposition. I briefly wondered if I shouldn't tell her a knock-knock joke to ease a bit of her concern. I certainly didn't like the fact that the tables seemed to have turned on us. "What happened to cause Jerry to up and leave a few weeks into the semester?"

"Professor Weaver, that's who happened." Cassandra straightened in the driver's seat in anger, looking at Piper and Orwin in the rearview mirror. I didn't have to worry about them getting out of the Jeep. They would take their cues from me, especially seeing as I was getting the full story from Cassandra. The last thing we wanted was to walk into this house unprepared. "Professor Weaver teaches a class in the occult. He's obsessed with vampirism and tales of the undead. It's basically his entire curriculum. At first, I thought maybe he had been born into a family of hunters. It didn't take long to figure out that he'd been searching for one of the undead for many years. With Jerry still learning to adapt to his heightened senses, it took exactly one day for our observant professor of the occult to figure out Jerry's secret."

"Professor Weaver wanted to be turned, didn't he?" I guessed, though it really wasn't presumption on my part. The underlying disgust in Cassandra's tone had pretty much said it all. It went beyond the pale that someone would actually want to drink blood on a daily basis to survive. Immortality was a falsehood, because there was nothing in nature that didn't have some type of weakness to end their reign here on earth...and that included Ammeline Letty Romilda. "I take it that Jerry refused Professor Weaver's somewhat adamant request."

Perhaps we could turn down the heat just a smidge? I'm becoming quite warm beneath my pristine white fur. And no, there is no need for the tables to be turned in the knock-knock joke department. I just need a few minutes to digest all this information, Miss Lilura. Right when I believed it couldn't get worse, this medium finds a way to twist the wooden stake a little deeper. That pun was completely intended.

"If Frank Palisade was telling the truth, which I'm quite certain he was, then Professor Weaver has to be the reason behind the bounty on Jerry's head." Cassandra bit her lip as if to keep her emotions in check. "It's quite well known that the professor has a vindictive streak over reviews left on those surveys done by the students, so I can only imagine the lengths he'd go to if someone turned down his delusion of immortality and becoming a vampire. We thought that maybe Professor Weaver would try and somehow go public or maybe tell a few of his online followers of the supernatural existence of vampires. That's why I was attempting to cloak the location of the cabin."

May I suggest talking over these types of dangerous decisions with your family, Miss Saruman? I'm sure that your parents would have warned you against getting involved with vampire business.

My phone vibrated in the pocket of my winter jacket. It didn't take me long to retrieve it, breathing a sigh of relief when Knox's name came across the display. He had texted that he had been back at the campsite and was currently headed into town. I quickly responded that we might need help, having Cassandra fill us in on the address of our location and promptly relaying it to Knox.

Did we not just discuss making precarious decisions in the heat of the moment? I'm not so sure bringing our resident werewolf to the home of a vampire is the best of ideas right now, dear hexed one. Werewolves are the bane of a vampire's existence.

"Look," Cassandra said after I'd slid the phone back into my pocket. She shifted until she was facing me. "I told you everything based on your word that you would help me keep Jerry safe. I need to know if I can still count on you. All this talk about werewolves, hexes, premonitions, and aliens has me concerned that you're not…well, I don't mean to throw around insults, especially given my recent circumstances."

I can see how we might come across as a bit eclectic, Miss Saruman. Rest assured, we are not the ones who've upset past generations with our actions. You are the responsible one.

"Pearl," I admonished, unable to believe that the one feline who was obsessed with etiquette would be so rude. "Cassandra is young, and she has a lot to learn. Let's just see what we can do to guarantee Jerry's safety, thereby helping Orwin to avoid those foreseen consequences."

I'd decided against sharing too much with Cassandra, but not for the obvious reasons. The less she knew about my hex and premonitions, the better. It was less likely that the future would unfold as seen in my vision.

As for Pearl, I'd already figured out that she had strong feelings with regard to our ancestors. Calling upon their power to aid the undead was a big no-no in the witchcraft world. Pearl was over two thousand years old, and she'd survived this long based on the promise of keeping those unwritten rules.

Miss Saruman, I don't suppose Mr. Kline's uncle has a spot of cream he could warm up in the microwave for approximately twenty-one seconds, would he?

Pearl was definitely out of sorts, but even she would agree with me that we couldn't allow Jerry Kline to meet his end at the sharp end of an oak stake.

It is rather tempting, is it not?

"My ancestors haven't completely abandoned me,"

Cassandra shared, realizing that neither Pearl nor I were going to reveal too much for the same reason we'd been wanting to meet with her. "If you need my help, I'll do the best that I can in return for your help in safeguarding Jerry."

"That's where Orwin comes in and saves the day." I reached for the door handle, prompting Cassandra to turn off the engine. It was time to get down to business so that we could get off this mountain in one piece. "Pearl, stick to him like glue."

It's a good thing I saw Mr. Cornelia take his allergy pill while at the diner. This is proving to be a very long day, indeed.

"What's going on?" Orwin asked cautiously, having vacated the Jeep and was now eyeing the one-story residence in front of us. He pushed his glasses up a bit in concern. "We're too close to these woods for my tastes, Lou. What if something goes wrong?"

By this time, Piper had joined us, as well as Cassandra. Pearl materialized, though she took everyone by surprise when she made herself comfortable on top of Orwin's right shoulder. He sneezed in under three seconds.

We need to take care of those pesky allergies, if you get my drift, alien hunter.

Pearl jumped down gracefully, the packed snow giving her a bit of cushion. She'd been extremely careful with revealing too much information about us, such as Orwin's lowering the protective ward he'd placed on himself months ago. We'd been so caught up in saving his life that we'd completely forgot about his allergies. Piper would have to take care of that the moment we had a few minutes to spare.

"Pearl will be by your side the entire time," I promised Orwin, ignoring Cassandra's skeptical glance. She'd probably put two and two together regarding our concern for Orwin's health and talk about my premonitions. Well, we were going to leave her wondering, because I wasn't confirming nor denying anything until seven o'clock tonight. "Orwin, is there a way for you to cast your particular brand of magic and take down that bounty on Jerry's head?"

I wasn't talking about witchcraft magic, but instead was referring to Orwin's ability to handle anything tech-related. Our first undertaking was to show Jerry we meant no harm. Removing the bounty on his head should accomplish that task, leaving Orwin safe and sound as a result. At least, for the time being.

An added bonus to this scenario is that this house isn't that big. We should technically all be able to stay within each other's sights, keeping watch over everyone.

"It might take me a while to access the backend of the app, using multiple probes on his existing communication ports, but I don't see why not. I have my laptop in the Jeep. Let me grab it."

"Jerry isn't going to hurt anyone." Cassandra's irritation that we thought otherwise was audible when she all but huffed her way past us toward the front door. No one moved until Orwin had retrieved his laptop, thus allowing Piper to lock the Jeep with a press of the key fob. She tossed me my keys, indicating that she believed all of us were walking away from this house with our lives intact. "Come on. Let me introduce you to Jerry before Sheriff Tate pulls up behind us. Jerry needs to know that you're all on our side, and also what story we told in order for him to relay the same timeline to the sheriff."

I never thought I'd see the day that my sweet Piper aided and abetted a vampire. Oh, I do so need a spot of warm cream to get me through the rest of this day.

Chapter Eleven

"I DON'T TRUST them," Jerry murmured warily, pulling Cassandra closer to his side as if we had ulterior motives. We did, but that was beside the point. The tables had somehow turned, and one of the undead now thought that we were the threat. "You shouldn't have brought them here, Cassie."

It's quite astonishing, isn't it? I finally understand Miss Saruman's defensive declaration regarding Mr. Kline's lack of murderous intent. Even after seven months, I'm not quite sure that Mr. Kline's mind has accepted what he has become or his relationship to his prey.

Pearl did have a diplomatic manner in how she described certain situations.

I'll take that as a compliment, dear hexed one.

I let Pearl have her moment while I carefully surveyed the living room and kitchen, which were only separated by a small island that didn't contain the usual stools. The open layout made it easier to keep track of everyone, which came in quite handy when we all needed to be within sight of Orwin. He was seated on the couch, his nimble fingers clicking away on the keyboard of his laptop as he searched for a way to remove the bounty on Jerry's head. Granted, it was a temporary solution, but it would solve our immediate problem.

Very true, dear hexed one. Where there is one hunter, there are more to follow.

"These people are the only reason that hunter left the mountain without his trophy," Cassandra reminded Jerry, having already explained the aftermath of his attack on Frank Palisade. She turned into Jerry's embrace, resting her hands gently on his chest. Every time she got too close to him, I couldn't help but brace myself for a display of fangs. If that were to happen, I needed to be ready to defend the rest of us. "Jerry, there is a bounty on your head. We thought for sure that Professor Weaver would do something, but a bounty? It's not like we have the option of going to the police and saying that someone is trying to kill you because you wouldn't turn him into a vampire. No one would believe a word we had to say."

"Cassandra's right." I stood near the front door, the location allowing me to position myself between the living room and the kitchen. Basically, I was ensuring that Jerry couldn't reach Orwin. The vampire would have to get through me first, and I was betting I was quicker on the draw given Jerry's lack of experience. "There are unwritten rules for the supernatural, Jerry. One of the most important is that we don't involve humans. Orwin is doing his best to make sure that the bounty on your head is removed before we quietly leave this mountain."

"Why would you do that?" Jerry wasn't so naïve, after all. "We don't know you. Cassie mentioned that you wanted to speak with her about her ability to contact your ancestors. You must need her help pretty bad to risk being involved in my problems."

"Cassandra already told us that those in the afterlife are upset by her decision to help you," Piper said from her seat next to Orwin. Hal occupied the recliner, but I'd seen him turn up his hearing aid so that he wouldn't miss a word of this conversation. He'd accepted what his nephew had become, and his actions already spoke to the lengths he'd go to in order to protect his family. "We understand that her powers as a medium are somewhat limited. Our offer to help you has no strings. If you'd like us to leave, we will. Then you can start preparing for the attack that is certain to come."

My sweet Piper is very good at negotiating, isn't she? I taught her myself, you know.

Pearl was in somewhat of a good mood after Hal had offered everyone a refreshment. We'd all declined, but Cassandra had made sure that Pearl had been given a spot of warm cream upon hearing the request multiple times over the course of the last couple of hours.

I did agree that Piper was our best bet to get Jerry to agree to our help. Her kindness practically radiated off her body, and the blonde curls falling around her face gave off an angelic vibe. It wasn't just her hands that had the ability to heal, but also her words.

"We need their help, Jerry," Cassandra whispered, grabbing onto his shirt so that he could see just how desperate she was to keep him safe. "I can't do this by myself."

Jerry pulled Cassandra close, his face way too adjacent to her neck for my liking. One bite was all it would take to sign her death sentence.

Has anyone ever mentioned to you that you have trust issues, dear hexed one?

"Don't start," I muttered, focusing my attention on Orwin. Pearl had witnessed my premonition. She understood completely why I was still uneasy. There was a clock on the far wall, and we still had a ways to go before seven o'clock. "Please tell me that you're close to deleting that bounty."

"I'm working as fast as I can. The university has an entire IT department and active monitoring of their firewall." Orwin continued to click away on his laptop, not bothering to look up from the screen. His glasses had slipped down the bridge of his nose, but he was so engrossed in what he was doing that it didn't seem to bother him. "Has anyone checked on the progress of that storm?"

"Should hit us sometime around six o'clock tonight," Hal chimed in warily as he gestured toward a small shortwave radio on the side table next to his recliner. He continued to stare at me guardedly, probably not quite sure what to think of us taking over his house. "Would the rest of you take a seat? No need to stand around twiddling your thumbs."

I like this man. He gets right to the point. Speaking of which, did anyone notice the wooden spike next to Mr. Hal's recliner?

"That's in case Paul decided to return without..." Cassandra allowed her words to trail off when Jerry and Hal both looked at her oddly. She'd already explained that she could hear Pearl's thoughts, but it was the first time she'd verbally carried on a conversation with the familiar. "Sorry. Pearl was wondering why you keep a stake next to your recliner, Hal."

"Paul had a temper before he was turned. His transition was a bit more difficult," Jerry reluctantly offered up, not joining us in the living room like his uncle would have preferred. Apparently, the trust issue went both ways. "Uncle Hal needs to take precautions."

I must say, Mr. Kline's intentions do seem pure. That isn't an adjective I would ever have thought would go hand in hand with one of the undead, but there you have it.

All this talk about Jerry being gentle and humane had me doubting that he was the one responsible for Orwin's death in my premonition. We'd assumed due to this morning's events that Jerry had been the one to bite Orwin, but maybe that wasn't the case. What if all along the vampire in question was Paul?

We could always have my sweet Piper scry for Mr. Paul

Kline's location. She does have the amethyst in her purse. I'm sure that there is something in this residence that belonged to Paul that could be used in the spell, thereby putting our minds at ease that he is far away from here.

"Yes, there is," Cassandra replied, stepping forward before Jerry could stop her. He had no idea what had been suggested, and he didn't like being left out of the conversation. "It's okay, Jerry. They can tell us where Paul is right this minute."

"Is that true?" Jerry asked before the sound of a car door closing could be heard through the front windows. Hopefully, it was Knox. "Paul used to live here with our uncle. Well, now it's just me. You can use something from Paul's bedroom. I'll talk to Sheriff Tate, sticking to the story that you told at the diner."

Piper quickly nodded, motioning for Pearl to join her in following Cassandra to the back of the house. The three of them had disappeared from sight by the time Jerry had answered the door. Hal had discreetly reached over the side of his recliner to push the wooden stake underneath the hanging fabric of the chair.

"Sheriff, I know I shouldn't have left the diner after having that altercation, but it was instinct. You've not been one of my biggest fans," Jerry said with a crooked smile, his charm coming across forced. Sheriff Tate didn't even break a smile. He tried again. "Cassandra told me that Mr. Palisade isn't going to press charges, for which I'm very grateful. My only excuse for throwing that weight was that I did so in self-defense. He got me confused with someone else, and I was afraid he was going to attack me."

"Jerry, don't say another word," Sheriff Tate warned, stepping inside and bringing a gust of cold wind with her. I noticed that the clicking on Orwin's laptop had come to a complete stop as he noticed the change in energy as well. Something bad had happened. As usual, whatever had occurred wasn't in the plans. "Have you been here since you left the diner? Can Hal or anyone else verify you were here?"

Sheriff Tate wasn't wearing gloves, and her bare hand rested on the butt of her firearm. I didn't get a sense of panic, as if she knew Jerry's deepest and darkest secret. No, her reaction was more in line with doing her job as sheriff while trying to protect a resident she didn't quite believe would resort to committing a serious crime.

"My nephew hasn't been out of my sight since we left the diner," Hal confirmed, pushing himself out of his recliner so that he could move to rest a hand on Jerry's shoulder. "What's going on, Sheriff?"

By this time, Orwin had closed his laptop and stood next to me. Cassandra, Piper, and Pearl must have also felt the shift of energy. Cassandra and Piper reappeared from the hallway, leaving Pearl to become invisible.

Something tells me that we should have thought to scry for Mr. Kline's brother before now, dear hexed one.

I didn't care for the fact that Knox had yet to join us,

and I clenched my hands tight as I waited for the sheriff to fill us in on the latest development. Did it involve another vampire, or had Knox somehow been discovered by the hunter we supposedly had sent back to wherever he belonged?

"Mr. Palisade was murdered in the room he'd rented above the bar," Sheriff Tate stated grimly, her gaze settling on each and every one of us until she focused her attention on Jerry. "You're the one who had an altercation with the man, Jerry. I'd like for you to come down to the station for more questioning. I had no choice but to call in the state police. They'll want to speak with you, and we should make their job as easy as we can by providing them with as much information as possible."

Oh, dear. This is a twist that we didn't see coming, dear hexed one.

That was putting things mildly. Who would want to see Frank Palisade dead other than Jerry? Was Paul closer than everyone thought? Was he the vampire who hurt Orwin in my premonition? No matter what happened in the next few moments, Piper had to stay behind to scry for Paul's location.

"I'll go with you," Cassandra volunteered blindly, unable to see that she might very well be putting herself in danger. I couldn't seem to get Pearl's warning out of my head—where one hunter went, another would follow. Frank Palisade hadn't been the only hunter to have knowledge of Jerry's whereabouts. Professor Weaver had made sure of that when anonymously posting the bounty on Jerry's head. "Hal?"

"Already grabbing my coat," Hal replied gruffly, his concern for his nephew palpable.

"I'm sorry, Cassandra," Sheriff Tate said, gesturing toward the rest of us now standing together in the living room. "I know your uncle is sick and that your brother came to take you back to see him. Hopefully, we'll be able to clear away the roads sometime tomorrow for all of you to be able to make it before it's too late."

Thankfully, Cassandra went along with the story we'd concocted. Jerry was holding up her dress coat in a gentlemanly fashion that would certainly score points with Pearl. All I could think of was that he hadn't fed on anything since we'd arrived, and there was no telling how long he'd be holed up at the police station.

That isn't quite accurate, Miss Lilura. During my little stroll to the back of the house, I noticed an empty blood bag in Mr. Kline's bedroom. I don't believe it was old, given the scent it left behind.

I scrunched my nose at Pearl's description, but at least we no longer had to worry that Jerry might lose it in an interrogation room. That is, if the small police station even had one of those. Right now, we had some hunting to do on this mountaintop.

"Hal, do you mind if we stay here?" I asked, hoping that Hal would understand the urgency to locate Paul. We had to be one hundred percent sure that he was nearby and could potentially be the one who murdered the vampire hunter. "I'm assuming the rooms above the bar are off limits now that the place is a crime scene."

"That would be best," Sheriff Tate replied reluctantly, stepping to the side so that she could keep Jerry in sight at all times. At least she hadn't put the man in cuffs. "I'm not sure how long the state police will have the bar closed off. They had Maggie shut down business for the day."

"Make yourselves at home," Hal relied, nodding in addition to his answer. He was letting me know that it was okay to still locate one of Paul's personal items for the locator spell. "We'll be back as soon as we clear up this mess."

No one spoke until Hal had closed the door behind him, leaving us to figure out who really killed Frank Palisade.

"Orwin, keep working on taking down that bounty," I directed, attempting to figure out how we could speed up the process of getting off this mountain with Orwin's life intact. "Piper, go back to Paul's room and find something that you can use to find his location. Pearl, consider yourself that glue you were talking about earlier. I'm going to find Knox."

You believe that our resident werewolf will need to be the hunter in this situation, do you not? Have you considered that Paul might not have come by himself? That bounty had to have spread throughout the vampire community. He might very well be here to protect his brother, not knowing that we have things under control.

"Yes, I've thought about that." My cell phone was in the pocket of my jacket, so I quickly crossed the room to the coat rack. "Which is why we'll be needing Knox in those woods if Piper finds Paul on top of this mountain. The last thing we need while ensuring Orwin's safety is a war between hunters and vampires, all because of a human's desire to be immortal."

Let's hope it doesn't come to that, dear hexed one. In the meantime, I will be glued to the alien hunter's side. It appears that in Mr. Palisade's death comes victory for Mr. Cornelia. It is time we had a little talk about the hieroglyphics in the pyramids that depict those little green visitors from the skies above.

"We're going to be hearing conspiracy theories for a long time to come, aren't we?" I asked with a small smile, somehow being the one to try and cut through the tension in the room. We were stuck in what could very well be an extremely dangerous situation that ended with my premonition. I really, really didn't appreciate the irony of it all. "At this point, I would give anything to hear those speculations about little green men."

Then we all best get to work, dear hexed one. There's no time to waste if we wish to all enjoy a Thanksgiving dinner next week. I, for one, am looking forward to giving thanks that Mr. Cornelia has yet to fit my sleek fur with an aluminum foil suit. Now, let's see if we can't go about saving the day, shall we?

Chapter Twelve

THE WIND HAD definitely picked up speed outside, if the groans of the one-story house were anything to go by, signifying that the impending storm would be arriving sooner rather than later. That didn't bode well for saving the day, let alone Orwin.

"I can hear you."

I lifted my right shoulder in chagrin, not having realized looking out the window of the living room had put me within mental thought of Orwin's position on the couch. It was going on five o'clock in the evening, leaving only two hours left on the premonition clock. Unfortunately, I hadn't been able to get ahold of Knox, Orwin had yet to take down the bounty on Jerry's head, and the incoming weather front was affecting Piper's ability to locate Paul.

"I can walk faster than the speed of this internet," Orwin complained, his fingers still clicking away on the keyboard.

"Maybe that's what we should have done," I surmised grimly, not liking how long we'd been waiting without any contact from the outside. Hal, Jerry, and Cassandra should have been back by now. "We should have gotten off this mountain first thing this morning and taken our chances in a place that isn't about to be snowed in for who knows how long."

Don't be such a negative Nelly, dear hexed one. We've managed to keep the alien hunter safe for this long. We can last two more hours. It is then that we'll be able to take a more offensive stance instead of the defensive one we've been forced to adopt.

"Maybe that's our problem," I muttered, wondering if by staying on the sidelines we'd taken the one path that could make my premonition come true.

"I can still hear you," Orwin exclaimed in disbelief, looking up from his laptop as he pushed his glasses a bit higher to get a better look at me. "You aren't helping my concentration any by constantly doubting our decisions. We're inside this house. If that changes, we'll worry about it then."

Mr. Cornelia does have a point there, Miss Lilura.

I moved to the other window on the opposite side of the front door, which still allowed me to keep watch of the front yard and gravel drive should Paul decide to pay his uncle and brother a visit. This way, Orwin couldn't hear my thoughts teetering back and forth while affording me to be the first line of defense.

"Pearl, I think I might have liked you better when you were thinking more like me."

I've since come to my senses, dear hexed one. Did you

know that witches are the barrier between humans and the supernatural realm? It is our duty to protect them. Having one of our own in danger sidetracked me for a tiny bit, but it wasn't anything a spot of warm cream didn't fix right up.

"Great," I said wryly, shifting the curtain a bit so that I could check the other side of the property. Dusk had fallen later due to the time change. Even though I'd turned on the porch light, it was getting harder and harder to see all the way to the edge of the cleared property line. "A familiar who—"

"I did it!" Piper exclaimed in victory, rushing down the small hallway. She'd been having quite a bit of trouble casting the locator spell due to the tempestuous elements in the air around us, so she'd moved to Paul's bedroom in hopes that any remaining essence of the man would aid in the success of the incantation. "Paul Kline is currently in a small town near Cody, Wyoming."

I must say that information is a bit surprising, my sweet Piper. The western part of Wyoming is home to many lycanthropes and their cousins, the Grey Wolf. I wonder what the young vampire is doing in those parts, unless he has a death wish, of course.

"We can't worry about Paul," I said, without the relief I thought would be entwined in those words. This discovery put us in another bind. To complicate matters further, my phone no longer had service. I did connect to the Wi-Fi briefly before Orwin just about had a coronary about me using up his precious bandwidth. My idea hadn't worked, anyway. Knox had no service, leaving us in a bit of a bind. "If Paul is nowhere near this mountaintop, then that only leaves other hunters who might very well kill one of their own for that bounty."

"Piper wasn't the only one successful in her mission," Orwin shared, beaming with pride. He held up his fists in victory. "I was able to remove the bounty in spite of the worst internet on the planet. Yes! I remain King of the Internet!"

"High-five, partner," Piper quipped, walking over and slapping Orwin's hand before she sat down in Hal's recliner. She glanced at her watch. "A little under two hours left before the premonition window closes. We've got this. Piece of cake."

I gave Orwin and Piper a moment to be proud of their accomplishments, not wanting to burst their little hope bubbles into a billion tiny little pieces. Unfortunately, we didn't have anything, especially a piece of cake.

"Let's see if we can put icing on that cake," Orwin said as he stretched out his arms and laced his fingers as if he were loosening up his muscles. He hadn't heard my thoughts on the subject of cake, seeing as I was still next to the front door. "I got to thinking that maybe Professor Weaver wasn't solely counting on vampire hunters to take out Jerry. What if Professor Weaver drove here himself to see if Jerry was part of some nest, thus giving him a broader opportunity to convince one of them to turn him?"

By that logic, Professor Weaver wouldn't be the guilty party in Miss Lilura's vision. I don't believe that someone who is that obsessed with vampirism would do anything to jeopardize his chance of becoming one of the undead. I, myself, don't see the appeal of that type of liquid diet. I'll stick to my delicious beverage of cream, thank you very much.

"It wouldn't hurt to rule Professor Weaver out of this equation," I surmised, becoming a bit uncomfortable with all these loose ends. "Unlike Paul, who ditched his cell phone and any type of technology that could lead us to him, at least you have Professor Weaver's cell phone number. Go ahead and pinpoint his location."

I'm not so sure that it's the multiple threads of this case that has you uncomfortable, dear hexed one. I also sense the shift in the air, and the dire awareness that things are about to take a turn is very palpable.

"I feel it, too. I thought it might be from the locator spell, but it's only becoming stronger," Piper said quietly, giving Orwin a sideways glance as he began to click away on his keyboard. "I realize that our current undertaking is to get past seven o'clock without Orwin meeting his maker, but we did promise to help Cassandra keep Jerry safe. If our cell phones have no service, then neither do the vampire hunters. They won't know that the bounty has been taken down until sometime tomorrow."

By then, it might be too late, my sweet Piper.

Hunters were turning on each other, all because of something far more evil than the dark side of the supernatural—money.

"It's a solo act," Orwin said with only the slightest sniffle and a shrug. He continued to work while giving a broader explanation. "Think about it. These vampire hunters travel the world alone in search for their prey. Most likely, the responsibility has been inherited from generations past. It's a dangerous and time-consuming hobby, leaving them questioning who to trust."

It's not like the vampires wear signs around their neck, Miss Lilura. It takes very good investigative skills to unearth the undead. A bounty such as the one Professor Weaver is offering can allow a hunter to pursue vampires for years to come without the need for some mundane job to support their habit.

"Professor Weaver isn't on this mountaintop," I declared before Orwin could confirm my suspicions. "Think about it. He had Jerry's address from his college application. The professor could have easily come here himself without the aid of any hunters. No, he put that bounty on Jerry's' head for revenge."

"You're right, Lou." Orwin finally closed his laptop. "Professor Weaver's cell phone is pinging at his residence near the college. I confirmed it was him through the camera on his computer."

"That's not a violation of privacy or anything," Piper said wryly, though she did appear quite relieved that there wasn't another player up on this mountain. "Remind me to put a piece of electrical tape over the camera on my laptop. So now what?"

I suggest we hunker down for the remaining time on that pesky premonition clock. What's the old saying? Better to be safe than sorry.

"Hal has a house phone," I said, looking back out the window of the front door. Flurries had begun to fall in those few short seconds I'd looked away from the edge of the tree line. By seven o'clock, we wouldn't be able to see past my red Jeep sitting in the driveway. "I'll call the police station to see if I can either get an update or request to speak with Cassandra."

It might be in our best interests to hold off until that timeframe closes and is sealed shut, dear hexed one.

"You don't think that Jerry, Cassandra, and maybe even Hal would have tried to skip town, do you?" Orwin asked, leaning forward so that he could set his laptop on the coffee table. He pushed up his glasses and leveled me a stare. "Honestly, that's what I would have done. Storm or no storm, it's in their best interest to go into hiding."

"It's not, though," Piper disagreed, resting an elbow on the arm of the recliner. "Remember, Jerry doesn't know that his brother isn't on this mountaintop. No one would take a chance getting caught in this storm with a vampire and a bunch of hunters on one's trail."

Lest we not forget that Mr. Kline would need access to those bags of blood in the refrigerator. He doesn't strike me as the type of vampire who would feed on his uncle or girlfriend, though I've been known to make a mistake a time or two in the past century.

"Really?" Orwin asked with a crooked smile, standing and stretching his legs. He'd been sitting in the same position for hours, moving only his fingers across the keyboard. "Can I mark this down on the calendar? Pearl Pippa Allifair admits she has been wrong on more than one occasion. That would look great on a plaque hung inside the RV. I could order it online."

You mean, alongside your aluminum foil hat? You would do well to recall that you removed the warding spell and that Piper has yet to rid you of your allergies. I might be tempted to curl up and fall asleep on your face, alien hunter.

Silence followed, and it carried on long enough that I finally looked away from the falling snow. Orwin and Piper were quietly exchanging glances while Pearl made a slight noise that I'm relatively sure was a gasp of horror.

"What?" I blurted out, already knowing that I wasn't going to like what they had to say. "Orwin?"

Orwin didn't reply. Instead, he took a deep breath before rubbing the back of his neck in worry.

I'll let you two deceivers deliver the bad news. Mr. Cornelia, how could you corrupt my sweet, sweet Piper? You purposefully distracted me with that spot of warm cream last night, didn't you?

"Hold up there, cotton ball. I didn't corrupt anyone," Orwin defended, though there did seem to be a bit of desperation in his tone. "There was a reasonable explanation as to why—"

"Everyone stop!" I practically yelled, garnering everyone's attention.

I'd been in such shock after deciphering from the three-way conversation that Orwin hadn't removed his protection ward, thus leaving him wide open to waltz right into death's door, that I hadn't moved. It was the only reason I'd caught the movement against the far edge of the tree line, past where my Jeep was parked in the gravel lane.

Knox's large frame had materialized from the swirling snowflakes and into the golden hue of the porch light…and he wasn't happy. I'd only ever seen that much rage written across his features once, and that was when we'd been surrounded by a pack of werewolves with our lives hanging in the balance.

Oh, dear. This can't be good, dear hexed one.

I didn't even reach for the doorknob. My ability to move things telekinetically responded, resulting in the door banging open hard enough that it was only happenstance the window hadn't shattered into a million pieces. My only thought was reaching Knox and making sure he wasn't hurt.

Is that a wooden stake in his hand, Miss Lilura?

My gaze instantly dropped down to the weapon he was holding in his right hand. Was that blood? I was still walking toward him as I quickly took in his appearance, finally noting that there was a hole in his jacket near his right shoulder.

Lycanthropes heal quickly, dear hexed one. Do not fear.

"Get back inside," Knox practically snarled through his clenched teeth. His eyes were maintaining a golden shimmer that I'd come to recognize as a sign. He wanted to turn. He wanted to unleash his inner beast on the individual who'd attacked him from afar. It wasn't something I'd ever pondered before, but I did wonder if Knox had allowed the person to live. "Now!"

Do as he says, dear hexed one. Quickly!

I instinctively backtracked, but not in fear of Knox or in response to Pearl's warning. Whatever had happened in order for him to be holding a stake dripping in blood was the reason he was barely hanging on to his human form, and I didn't take that lightly. I had no idea what the outcome had been in response to an attack. Until I had the facts, Orwin's life was still in danger.

Mr. Cornelia is safe for now, dear hexed one.

Pearl and Piper must have hurried to stand in the doorway when I'd bolted outside, for they needed to quickly scramble backward in order to let me inside. Orwin had his back against the corner of the room, lowering a crossbow that he'd brought inside with him earlier today.

"Knox, what happened?"

He'd all but slammed the door closed behind him, the intensity of his heated gaze telling us that he was in full control. He held up the wooden stake in a tight grip for all of us to see, in spite of what pain he might be experiencing from his injury.

"Someone thought it was a wise idea to stake me," Knox growled, his words rumbling deeper the longer he spoke. "Bad idea. I'm done scouting the area for that cabin, Lou. It's time that the hunters become the prey."

I daresay someone might have poked the bear...or wolf, in this case.

Chapter Thirteen

"KNOX, LET ME take a look at your shoulder," I directed once he'd handed off the thin oak bolt to Orwin. It was actually a classic crossbow bolt and round with two fins, with one flat end and the other pointed, for maximum penetration to the target. "Piper can heal you while we make a plan."

I had no choice but to push away my concern that Orwin was currently vulnerable to death by not lowering that protection spell he'd had in place against Ammeline. We had to deal with each problem one by one, and Knox topped that list by having been attacked by a vampire hunter. If he changed into his wolf form, the wound would heal instantly.

I'd like to know how the pursuer escaped with his or her life. It's clear that our resident lycanthrope is itching to turn the tables. And yes, dear hexed one, that pun was clearly intended.

"I'm fine," Knox responded, taking my hand in his when I'd tried to guide him to the kitchen. He took a deep breath and even squeezed my fingers in reassurance.

"Really. I'm fine. The wound will be gone by morning even without turning."

"Why wait until morning?" Piper asked, having more success in shooing Knox to the kitchen. He dropped my hand when it was evident that Piper wasn't going to take no for an answer. "Remove your jacket so I can see the extent of your injury."

I purposefully didn't follow the two of them, wanting a moment alone with Orwin.

Not quite alone, dear hexed one. I want in on this conversation. I have a few choice words to say to Mr. Cornelia as well.

"Does this mean you care about me, Q-tip?" Orwin asked, though he was unable to keep the tremor out of his tone when Pearl and I remained silent. He held up the stake in surrender. "Fine. The both of you want answers. Well, I don't have them. I had every intention of lowering the protection ward I'd cast against Ammeline, but we ran into a bit of a problem. I made Piper promise not to tell you, because I knew you'd only get upset and freak out."

"Pearl, do I look like I'm freaking out?" I asked, clipping my words on purpose. I was now afraid and angry, but most of all hurt. "And here I considered myself a very level-headed individual."

Mr. Cornelia, may I suggest putting that shovel down that you keep digging that hole you're in at the moment? You somehow got Piper to deceive not only a friend, but her very own familiar. That does not go unanswered, alien hunter. You might wake up with green hair.

"No one deceived anyone," Orwin objected, though his protest came across rather weak. "We just didn't want you to worry when there wasn't anything anyone can do."

"What do you mean that there wasn't anything anyone can do? In case you've forgotten, we have a healer in our presence. How is Piper going to heal you if my premonition comes to fruition?"

You have access to an online dictionary, alien hunter. You should know better than to split hairs, especially when those blonde strands belong to my sweet Piper. You make it very hard for me not to cave under my instinct of curling up a ball and suffocating you in the middle of the night.

Orwin had walked into that one all on his own. He knew of Pearl's underlying tendency to be rather merciless when it came to defending Piper. Making her believe that it was alright to lie to us was wrong on every level.

"I can hear you," Orwin said with exasperation, sitting down on the couch as he held on to the stake. "But you need to put yourself in my shoes. Knox has been out scouring this mountain for the same cabin I stumbled in during your vision. Pearl has been by my side for the last twenty-two hours, and you're doing everything in your power to make sure your premonition doesn't come true. Adding pressure that I couldn't be healed if something went wrong with our plan would have only put the two of you on edge more than you already are."

My sweet Piper purposefully hid her thoughts from me, Mr. Cornelia.

I had a feeling that I was going to forgive Orwin a lot faster than Pearl, but we were both going to have to deal with the repercussions of their choices later. Orwin was now vulnerable in a way we hadn't anticipated, which meant protecting him had become even more imperative then before.

I'm second-guessing that, dear hexed one. Have you considered that maybe I was the guilty party in your vision? I do keep my claws rather sharp when it comes to one's reckoning.

"It's not like I convinced Piper to rob a bank on the side," Orwin exclaimed in defense of himself, managing to only continue to dig that proverbial hole deeper. "Cut me some slack. I just didn't want either of you to worry."

Isn't that for us to decide, alien hunter? Don't think for a moment that I can't summon those little green men of yours.

"Why couldn't you lower your protection ward, Orwin?" I asked, wanting to get to the root of the problem. Maybe there was a way we could get around that matter now that we could put our minds together. Orwin's conspiracy obsessions were tempting him to latch onto Pearl's bait, but the truth wouldn't matter if he ended up dead. "No spell is permanent, so what do we have to do to reverse it?"

"That's just it. To reverse the spell, it has to be done

with the same material components, same weather conditions, and in the same location as where the incantation was cast." Orwin sighed in defeat, leaning back against the couch. At least he was careful not to put the bloody stake down onto the fabric. "And last I checked, we were nowhere near California."

Pearl continued to narrow her emerald green eyes his way, as if debating on whether or not to keep lecturing him on his decision to keep us in the dark. I completely understood her anger and resentment at pulling Piper into his cover story, but everyone needed a loyal friend.

"Please don't make me feel worse about lying to you than I already do," Orwin beseeched us as he held up the stake that a hunter seemed so inclined to somehow put into Knox's shoulder. I was wondering how a human could get close enough to a werewolf to pull off something of that magnitude, but first we needed to sort out this lying business. "No, we don't need to sort out anything. I was wrong, Lou. I shouldn't have asked Piper to keep something so important from you or Pearl, regardless that I was just trying to stop you from worrying about something we might not be able to control. As for how a hunter was able to stab a werewolf with a stake, this particular wooden post is meant for a very special crossbow."

I'm still waiting for my apology, alien hunter. My sweet Piper is my charge, after all.

"Piper is the most compassionate, kind, and loyal

friend anyone could ever ask for, Pearl. I know that wasn't only her parents doing, and I truly am sor—"

That's good enough, alien hunter. Apology accepted. I reserve the right to smother you in your sleep should you do something so foolish as this again in the future. Fair warning—not even those green little men would be able to save you. Now, I fear that our dear hexed one is having a moment.

"I'm not having a moment," I countered, but the vision of someone trying to kill Knox fueled my anger. I'd always considered myself responsible for those who'd joined me on this quest. As Pearl had so eloquently stated, we were the only ones who got to murder each other. "The hunter shot at Knox from a distance. The huntsman has no idea what Knox truly hides underneath the surface."

Mr. Kline's pursuers instinctively guessed wrong that our resident werewolf was one of the undead. Foolish mistake. Amateurs hunters.

"There is some type of engraving on the end of the bolt," Knox said, walking back into the living room as he pulled his t-shirt back over his head. I couldn't help but count, and now I was relatively sure there was such a thing as an eight pack. "It's almost like an insignia of some sort."

I held out my hand to look at the stake myself, ignoring the knowing looks I was receiving from Orwin and Pearl. Speaking of foolish mistakes, thoughts were easily misinterpreted. I had merely been considering the health benefits of being a werewolf, nothing more.

"Don't make me use this," I muttered to both Orwin and Pearl, who wisely remained silent. I studied the flat end of the bolt, the emblem easy to make out as it had been branded into the wood. Someone had spent a lot of time fashioning these stakes. "Whoever is hunting Jerry wants the other hunters to know who is responsible for taking him out."

This type of mark would make sense, given that evidence was needed in order to collect a bounty. Professor Weaver had taken a chance that Jerry, Paul, or another vampire wouldn't attempt some type of retaliation. Unless the professor was being protected by other hunters. Presuming we got Jerry out of this situation alive, we'd allow him and Cassandra to neutralize the good ol' professor.

"Orwin, did you explain what happened when we attempted to lower your protection ward?" Piper asked, her concern over our reactions appropriate. No more lies, and that meant Orwin would eventually have to reveal the truth as to why he'd joined me on this venture. "I'm not sorry that I kept my word to a friend."

Of course, you're not. My sweet Piper, loyalty is a rare quality these days. Mr. Cornelia and I have come to an agreement, and he shall not put you in such a position again. Isn't that right, alien hunter?

"Pearl, no smothering," Piper warned with a know-ing smile. Either that or she was just grateful that we weren't going to carry a grudge about being kept in the dark. "Now, Knox is healed. Good as new. We have to figure out our next plan. I'm thinking we call the station and find out what is taking Jerry, Cassandra, and Hal so long to return."

"The four of you should stay here." Knox's eyes still contained that golden shimmer. The rage that had consumed him upon being staked lay just below his feigned composed appearance. He wanted to hunt, and for very good reason. "I'm done playing the amateur sleuth."

"I don't think that's such a good—"

Knox held up his hand, tilting his head toward the back of the house. He'd heard something that the rest of us hadn't, which wasn't surprising given his abilities. We all remained quiet, watching as Knox quietly made his way to the back of the house. I motioned for everyone to stay together while I followed close behind, ready and willing to fight alongside of Knox if it came down to it.

"Get out," Knox ordered, turning abruptly on those military boots of his before I could stop myself from running into him. His hands were on my arms, turning me around without hesitation. "Now. Go!"

I certainly didn't dawdle. If there was a stake that was about to come crashing through one of the bedroom windows at lightning speed, I didn't want to be in the crosshairs.

"Someone set the house on fire. I can smell the

smoke. Get everyone out of here," Knox ordered, pushing everyone so that he could take a look out the front window. "Be careful getting to the Jeep, and drive straight to the police station. I'll meet you there."

May we pause for just a moment, colleagues? The hunter or hunters who thought our resident werewolf was a vampire has clearly decided to force us out from the safety of Mr. Kline's house. There is no safe passage once we exit through that front door, dear hexed one.

"I know that, but what choice do we have?" I asked, beginning to smell the smoke from whatever had been set on fire. "The hunters have forced our hand."

"Pearl is going to have to buy us some time." Piper had secured her body purse and picked up Orwin's laptop to hold close to her chest. She kissed Pearl on top of the head. "Stay invisible and be careful. Knox, you're going to need to protect Orwin until we make it to the Jeep."

I will cause the most epic of distractions, my sweet Piper.

Pearl vanished, allowing Piper to join Orwin as she laced their fingers together in support.

"I'll pull up to the back and do my best to dislodge any stakes that are aimed in our direction." I was comfortable with this plan, though it would take a lot of concentration. One thing about Knox's comment regarding all of us meeting at the station didn't sit right with me. "Knox, we're all in agreement, right?"

"Not quite." Knox looked over his shoulder where the smoke was starting to billow in the hallway. I could have attempted to push it back, but that would only have bought us a couple of seconds. We needed to leave now. "I have a bit of hunting to do."

I didn't worry that Knox would do something unethical. He wouldn't actively seek someone out to kill them, regardless that it was in the nature of his beast. He'd tamed what he could of the lycanthropy that had been bestowed upon him, but that didn't mean his werewolf side didn't like to come out to play every now and then.

"Knox, now isn't the time to even the playing field," I reminded him, grabbing onto his jacket so that he'd know I meant business. "We need to stay together."

By this point, even I could hear the crackling of the fire as it devoured the rear walls of the house. We had needed to give Pearl time to cause a distraction, but it was best if we left now. Knox stopping long enough to give me a charming smile hadn't been in the cards.

"Worried about me, Lou?" Knox winked at me. I mean, he actually winked at me as if we were just about to take a stroll through the park instead of being shot at by crossbows. It took a lot to make me speechless. "I won't go getting myself killed if that's what you're worried about. At some point, I'd really like to share a drink while you tell me that story regarding your coven. See you soon, sweetheart."

Knox actually exited through the front door as if he were going for an evening stroll through the falling snow. I'm pretty sure I was beyond speechless. He chose now, the most dangerous situation we'd ever been in, to flirt.

"Wow. Wait until Pearl hears about this," Orwin muttered in what sounded suspiciously like glee. He realized his mistake right away. "Hey, I'm just a witness. Can we get out of here now? Pearl most assuredly has things under control out there, and now she has Knox as backup."

I muttered a few choice words under my breath after snatching my coat before grabbing Orwin's arm and positioning him behind Piper. As planned, I'd pull up the rear. The best course of action was to assume Knox had been playful before he left so that none of us would overly worry about him being hurt while turning the tables on the hunter who'd tried to kill him.

"Can we evaluate my love life later, please?"

"I'm so glad I can't read minds," Piper murmured right before she flung open the door. The biting cold wind hit us directly in the face, but Piper ignored its warning. "Keep your head down!"

I flipped the porch light off right before we exited the house, purposefully making it difficult for a hunter to see our progress to the Jeep. The fire was in the back of the house, so the shadows should keep us safe until reached the refuge of my vehicle. Hopefully, there was only one hunter to deal with in this situation. If that was the case, he was most likely busy trying to figure out what was making noise in the forest behind him while worrying about Knox coming from the front. I had to have faith in the plan.

"Well, you might want revise that plan," Orwin whispered in horror after I'd all but smashed my face into his back. He wasn't the one who had stopped so abruptly, though. "The tires are slashed on all the vehicles, and I don't see Knox's Land Rover."

I figured we had a little over an hour until the timeframe on my premonition expired. The heart of town was about a mile to the west of us, but we couldn't take the chance of walking on the main road. We were left with little choice but to enter the very woods where the one cabin was located that we needed to avoid at all cost.

Chapter Fourteen

"Go," I URGED, keeping a lid on my panic so that it didn't come through my directive. Hopefully, Orwin would be too busy with his own apprehension to notice mine. "Piper, head for the woods. We'll go on foot. Whatever you do, don't let go of Orwin's hand."

It was hard not to wince every time I could hear a shift in the cold air or a branch snap far away from our location. I kept expecting a wooden stake to be shot from a crossbow, hitting me square in the back before I had the chance to deflect the weapon. High alert wasn't going to be enough when we were scrambling for safety. Hopefully, Pearl and Knox were successful in their attempt at distracting the hunter who'd all but flushed us out of our safety net.

"Unless there is more than one," Orwin muttered, a bit out of breath. He wasn't out of shape in the least. Our difficulty in drawing air had to do with the bitter cold air hitting the lining of our lungs. "We should have cast a spell to get those tires inflated."

"It would have taken too long," I replied, keeping

watch over my shoulder for any sign that we were being followed.

Piper remained silent as she led the way, only calling out when a branch was hanging too low. She was leading us toward the main road, hurtling through the woods at a rapid pace. We would stay hidden just inside the edge of the wood line.

A large shadow appeared to our right, and I instinctively lifted my arm and pushed as much energy as I could with the palm of my hand. The grunt of pain was low enough that it didn't echo through the trees, but just enough to know that I'd hit my target.

Your target just so happened to be our resident werewolf, who has successfully thwarted a hunter attack. We're safe for now, dear hexed one.

Piper, Orwin, and I all pulled up short at Pearl's sudden appearance. She was sitting on a fallen log that was protected from the snow by the trees above, looking serene as usual and without a hair out of place.

"When you say thwarted, you mean…" Orwin basically fed the question to Pearl, hoping beyond hope that she didn't mean it was Knox who'd enjoyed an evening snack.

Mr. Emeric didn't need to shift, if that's what you're asking, alien hunter. He simply used his military skills to disarm the man, threaten his life, explain that the bounty had been lifted, and then send the huntsman on his merry way with a kick to the rear.

I'd heard enough to know that we had nothing to

worry about in terms of a vampire hunter going into an online chatroom reserved for the like and outing the werewolf species. For now, lycanthropes remained nothing more than a myth in the eyes of the human realm. I quickly made my way the thirty feet or so to where Knox had landed on the ground with a thud. By the time I was standing over him, he'd rested his right hand across his chest where he must have felt the energy I'd hurled his way.

"Miss me?"

"Stop that," I directed, instinctively leaning down and scanning his face for any sign of damage that I may have caused. "Did you break anything?"

"I'm a werewolf, Lou," Knox said, as if I needed the reminder. His eyes still contained that golden hue that clued me in that he wasn't as relaxed as he made himself out to be. Even so, his five o'clock shadow did nothing to hide his smile. "Although, I could definitely get used to all this attention."

Maybe if I'd had Orwin's ability to read minds, I could decipher what had changed in the last twenty-four hours that had Knox go from being this intense lycanthrope with a thirst for revenge to this charming man who was clearly directing his wiles at me. I shook my head in disbelief and was about to stand up when he caught my arm.

"The hunter didn't know that Jerry had been taken to the police station." Knox lifted himself until he was resting an elbow in the wet foliage. Even the thick vegetation above wasn't enough to stop the snow from sneaking past the wide branches. "He'd arrived after the fact. For the last couple of hours, he'd been canvassing the back of the property in an attempt to lure Jerry out of the house. He thought the silhouettes he saw through the blinds were Jerry and his uncle."

Knox finally motioned that he was ready to lift himself off the wet ground. I stood back and gave him space, wondering just how much information Knox had been able to collect in that short amount of time. It was better focusing on our current situation than why Knox suddenly had a change in personality.

Our resident werewolf hasn't had a change of personality, dear hexed one. He is simply showing his true self after having had a conversation with my sweet Piper. Now, may we please continue our trek into town? My paws are quite wet, and you know I don't enjoy moist paws, cold or otherwise.

"Pearl, you're not telling Lou all my secrets, are you?" Knox asked, brushing off what dirt he could from his jeans. I inhaled deeply—though how I didn't go into a coughing fit from the bitter cold, I'll never know—and counted to five so that my irritation didn't catch his attention. Knox continued. "Listen, I wasn't always overly serious and distant. My run in with Ammeline stole my life, my family, and basically my identity. Piper couldn't sleep last night, and she just reminded me that Ammeline would continue to win every single day if I allowed this curse to take away what makes me…well, me. I'm still on this quest with you, because I'd like to think one day we could finally rid the world of an insane individual whose mind is basically rotting into a void of madness. At the same time, she is destroying people's lives."

"And you chose now to be…carefree?" I asked, unable to stop myself from commenting on this ludicrous discussion. I mean, we were running from a huntsman in the middle of a snowstorm on top of a mountain. It didn't help that the premonition clock was still ticking away. "Never mind. I didn't ask that question. We need to keep moving. Where is your Land Rover?"

I daresay you seem a bit flustered, dear hexed one.

"Hush it, cotton ball," I muttered, taking a page out of Orwin's book. "We need to make it safely to town, far away from any cabins that Orwin might stroll into in the next half hour or so. We'll find Knox's Land Rover and then head back into town to see what's going on at the police station. We should be safe there for the time being."

I'm not one for those horror flicks, dear hexed one, but I'm pretty sure those are the types of phrases that are said by the person who gets chopped up first.

"It's not like we have any other choice."

I smelled the smoke hanging heavy in the air as the cold wind twirled around us. We'd already ventured deep into the woods, but there were times I'd catch sight of the orange blaze if I were to stand just right.

I hadn't had time to put on gloves before we'd left the house, but at least they were tucked inside my pocket for later use. Truthfully, I didn't like wearing them when there was a very good chance I'd have to use magic, but standing still in the freezing cold had me changing my mind. The bitter wind seemed to have found the perfect path to weave its way through the forest.

"There's no way we're getting my Land Rover out of that ditch," Knox warned, walking around Orwin and Piper to take the lead through the dense woods. "There's also a chance the tire rod busted when I veered into a downed tree."

Please relay to our resident werewolf that is nothing a spot of magic can't cure.

"Nothing we can't fix," Orwin translated, seeming to finally notice that we'd once again put him in the middle of our lineup. He only ever got really quiet when he was nervous about something. And rightly so, given there was still minutes left on his life. Still, he offered up his two cents. "Knox, you mentioned the hunter thought Jerry and Hal were inside the house. Does anyone else find it odd that a vampire hunter, whose very life depends on their ability to hunt, didn't notice the different-sized silhouettes or the fact that there were more than two people inside the residence?"

"It crossed my mind." Knox had been able to guide us close to the road, though he still stayed within the edge of the tree line to give us some type of cover. He continued to venture parallel to the now snow-covered thoroughfare, explaining in a bit more detail the brief conversation he'd exchanged with the hunter. "He said his name was Nick Howell, and he was definitely dressed for the weather. I'm relatively sure that by the time Pearl and I got done with him, he headed for whatever hole he crawled out of to collect the bounty on Jerry's head."

"He won't get far in this weather," Piper said softly, stepping in the same spot as Knox had with his boots to maintain the illusion of only one person walking through the woods. "The snow is coming down in record time."

Ask Mr. Emeric about the stakes Mr. Howell had in his possession, dear hexed one.

"Knox, was there anything special about Nick Howell's stakes?" I asked with curiosity, wondering why he hadn't mentioned something that could affect the outcome of my premonition.

"Pearl, not nice to rat me out. I thought we were friends." Knox finally came to a stop. We were still quite a ways from town. I could only assume his Land Rover was somewhere close. "I didn't want any of you to worry more than you already were. I'll take care of it once we get into town."

I wouldn't suggest that bit of vengeance, dear hexed one. You see, Mr. Emeric's inner wolf might have taken it a bit personally when he was shot with that crossbow. He's a bit irritable over it, if you must know.

"Take care of what?" Orwin asked cautiously, pushing up his glasses even thought they were covered with water spots from the snow. He retrieved his phone from his pocket to check the time. "There's twenty minutes before I can breathe a little easier, but I'd rather know what I'm facing in those twenty minutes."

"Spill it," I exclaimed, noticing that it was becoming harder and harder to spot Pearl. Her white fur literally matched the white snow falling all around us now that we were next to the road. "Knox, what did you find out?"

"It could be nothing," Knox said, motioning for us to carefully cross the road. Our winter boots helped with traction, especially since the snowplows hadn't reached this part of the area. The cover of the woods had made it hard to see just how bad the storm had become. Now? I had no doubt that whoever had been on this mountain an hour ago would still be here come tomorrow morning. The last thing we needed was to bring a supernatural war to the residents of this small town. "There's my baby. I've seen all of you do magic before, but getting my Land Rover out of that ditch might take a miracle and a couple of werewolves."

Please relay to Mr. Emeric that we specialize in miracles, and we're very good at our jobs. We're still attempting to get Miss Lilura to lighten up a bit, but that's a work in progress.

Orwin saw fit to actually convey Pearl's sentiment, though I'm pretty sure it was just to keep his mind off the imaginary timer ticking down. It wasn't like we had time to waste, though. I left everyone standing on the side of the road, carefully making my way down the ditch. By the time I'd finagled my way through the accumulated snow and downed branches, I'd gotten my hands soaking wet and half-frozen.

The elements weren't ideal when using magic, but it did mean I was able to harness more energy directly from the elements. The falling snow started to swirl even more as I began to draw the power of the earth into my body and through the palms of my hands. Most times, I was able to flick the current from one arm. A damaged, jammed vehicle was another thing altogether.

The squeal of metal against the tree echoed throughout the woods, bouncing from tree to tree until the piercing sound faded in the distance. Inch by inch, I was able to shift the Land Rover until it was just inches from the road.

Very well done, dear hexed one. Now that the current mission has been accomplished, may I suggest asking our resident werewolf once again about his recent discovery.

The heat in the palms of my hands had intensified to the point of discomfort. The soft fabric in the inside of my gloves were somewhat of a relief when I was able to slide them back over my sensitive skin. It was time to follow Pearl's advice, and I finally began to make my way back up the trench only to find that Knox had followed me at a close distance. He'd been my eyes and ears, protecting me from anything or anyone who might have witnessed my magic.

"Your abilities never cease to amaze me," Knox said with a lopsided grin. Being a lycanthrope, his body heat was higher than an average person's. Even so, his cheeks and nose were tinged with a touch of rouge from the cold. "Remind me not to make you mad."

"Then tell me what it is you're hiding from me." My responsibility to keep Orwin alive far outweighed whatever flirtatious thing Knox had going on, so I grabbed ahold of his jacket before he could walk back within distance of Orwin's ability. "Knox, what did you find out from that hunter?"

"The stakes the huntsman had in his bag were plain." Knox wasn't wearing gloves, and his habit of rubbing his five o'clock shadow hinted at his concern of the situation. "Literally. There was no brand anywhere in the wood. Whoever shot me earlier was not the same hunter as the one who lit Hal Kline's house on fire. Speaking of which, I can hear the firetruck sirens. They'll be heading this way soon. Unfortunately, I'll need to change that flat tire before we can head into town."

As suspected, dear hexed one, there are other hunters lurking about these woods. The faster we get our buttocks in town, the better.

"Lou," Piper called out from near the front of the Land Rover. She was waving her hand for us to come to her quickly. "Lou, do you hear that? Fire trucks."

The sirens became louder and louder, responding to a call from someone about the fire at Hal's place. The neighbors around this area had a lot of space between their lands, but someone must have seen the orange blaze. The smell of smoke was also heavy in the air.

"Orwin and Piper, can you use a spell to get that tire temporarily fixed for us to reach town?" I asked as we got a bit closer to the rest of the group. "We shouldn't waste time."

"It's not only the firetrucks headed this way," Knox murmured, coming to stand close to me. His body protected me from the wind.

It seems that Sheriff Tate and the state police had to release Mr. Kline on account of his alibi. We now have a choice to make. Fulfill our promise to keep Mr. Kline safe from the hunters who lurk in these woods...or head into town where Mr. Cornelia is safe and sound. What shall it be, dear hexed one?

Chapter Fifteen

T HE TWO FIRETRUCKS, followed by Jerry's vehicle, passed by the Land Rover on the way to Hal's residence. I somehow managed to catch Cassandra's gaze. She seemed okay, maybe even a bit relieved. Her response alone told me that the state police didn't have any evidence to keep Jerry in custody any longer.

"Not every hunter has been made aware of the fact that the bounty was removed from Jerry's head," Piper said once she was able to be heard over the fading sirens. She motioned for Orwin to quickly join her next to the flat tire. "We need to move fast."

That we do, my sweet Piper. Have we decided to head into the safety of town, or are we driving back to the scene of the crime in order to fulfill our promise to keep Mr. Kline safe?

"I'm thinking we split up," I responded after careful consideration. "Piper and Pearl, you take the Land Rover back to town. Hole up in the room above the bar. Maybe the state police have cleared the crime scene. I figure there's probably a few minutes left on the premonition clock, but I'd rather get in a few more hours just to be safe. In the meantime, Knox and I can walk back to Hal's place. I'm sure it will take the firefighter some time to get that blaze under control."

That sounds like a brilliant plan, dear hexed one, although I'm not quite certain that Mr. Emeric is on board.

Sure enough, Knox had retreated to the spot where I'd been standing to peer into the darkness. His black hair held the remnants of snow, which melted slightly faster on him than it did the rest of us.

"Knox?" I had planned on walking to him, but I could make out another set of headlights coming from the direction of town. Who would be crazy enough to drive around in this weather unless forced to? "Someone else is heading our way."

Perhaps a hunter. Step back from sight, alien hunter. No one other than me is permitted to torment you.

"Someone else is in these woods," Knox conveyed with concern, not hearing Pearl's directive. His silhouette was quite dark against the backdrop of the forest, but the golden shimmer of his gaze was still recognizable. "We have company."

Uninvited, I might add. I abhor rudeness.

I had a split second to make a decision.

That you do, dear hexed one. Make it snappy.

"Go," I directed Knox, not wanting to be standing out in the middle of nowhere longer than necessary. "I'll meet you at Hal's place, and then we'll hitch a ride with them when they decide to drive back to town. It's not like they have anywhere else to stay."

Knox didn't say another word and simply faded into the dark void to do what he did best—hunt.

I shall stick to Mr. Cornelia's side like glue, dear hexed one. Have no worries.

"It's the sheriff," Orwin said with slight relief, still not through finishing the spell with Piper. They had both stopped chanting underneath their breath to come stand beside me. The last thing we needed was for us to look suspicious. "She must be driving to the fire."

I wasn't surprised when the sheriff's vehicle stopped beside the Land Rover, which was still somewhat close to the ditch. Orwin and Piper stayed where they were, with Pearl by Orwin's side in her invisible state.

"Is everything okay here?" Sheriff Tate asked through the rolled-down passenger window. Her blue gaze searched mine for the truth. "Were you at Hal's place when it caught fire?"

Trick question, dear hexed one. Tread carefully.

"No, ma'am." I pulled my right glove a little higher on my wrist as I leaned down to rest my arm against the open window frame. "It seems someone slit all four of my tires. We called a friend, and he was able to pick us up. Unfortunately, he hit some packed snow. We're just going to change this tire as fast as we can before heading back into town."

"Friend?" Sheriff Tate asked, searching the dark void behind me. I knew for a fact that she'd only see Orwin and Piper. "Is he okay? Was he hurt when he ran off the road?"

Time to bring this gathering to a close, Miss Lilura. I don't like how she is searching the area for Mr. Emeric.

Pearl hadn't needed to say anything in the way of a warning. The suspicion in Sheriff Tate's tone all but told me that it was time to wrap this conversation up as quickly as possible. I'm sure she already found the entire day odd, especially after finding the dead body of the man Jerry had attacked with a weight scale.

Do we need to mention that the true hunters in this area haven't seen any wildlife recently? Or that one of the local residents—Mr. Paul Kline—all but up and left his family and friends without even a simple goodbye? Sheriff Tate isn't a fool, dear hexed one. She knows more about this town than probably anyone else.

I completely agreed with Pearl's analysis, but I couldn't take the chance of having Orwin move closer to read Sheriff Tate's thoughts...not with Knox literally hunting someone who was currently lurking in the woods behind us.

"No, he's fine," I responded with a small smile, not willing to give up Knox's name. I had no idea what Sheriff Tate might do with the information, and the weather was making a turn for the worse. As a matter of fact, I could barely stop my teeth from chattering. "We're just going to change this flat tire and head back into town, but maybe I could get a ride with you to Hal's place. I can get a ride back to town with Cassandra. I'm sure she'll want to get an early start on the road after this storm passes."

"Why don't you all hop in the car?" Sheriff Tate suggested, motioning to the road in front of her. "I'll give you a lift. As your friend just experienced, these roads are treacherous. You can fix both vehicles come tomorrow."

Why does that offer feel like a trap? I'd rather stay out in this snowstorm than get in that vehicle, dear hexed one. Trust your instinct and—duck!

Had I not been talking with Sheriff Tate and wasting time by attempting to throw her off our trail, I would have realized that the air had shifted in the last few seconds. It was a wonder that Pearl had noticed, seeing as she had been midsentence.

The sound of a thud, like something hitting the Land Rover, carried off into the wind.

"Orwin!" Piper called out after he'd emitted what sounded like a groan of pain. There was no one else present, so I wasn't worried that he'd been bit by a vampire. "Are you okay?"

I quickly ran over to where they were standing in front of Knox's vehicle, noticing right away the wooden stake sticking out of the grill. Someone had a crossbow, but it was too dark to tell if it was the previous hunter that Knox had his run-in with or someone else entirely.

A vicious growl emanated from deep within the forest.

Whoever it is just might be about to meet their competition, but we might have a problem of our own to deal with, Miss Lilura. Please turn around slowly, so as not to startle Sheriff Tate. I don't appreciate the way the town officials welcome tourists in this town.

The sound of the police cruiser's door opening after I'd run to Orwin's side was unmistakable, but no more so than the noise Sheriff Tate made when removing her firearm from its holster. Oh, this put us in quite the bind.

"Don't move," Sheriff Tate warned as I finally faced her. "Emily? Are you out there? What was that sound?"

Emily?

"Her daughter," Orwin murmured, lifting a hand to his neck. My heartrate spiked when I realized that he was bleeding from the side of his neck. It had been just like my vision, only without the cabin. "Emily Tate is a hunter, Lou. She was the young woman who was reading at the diner. It's her stakes that have the insignia."

Mr. Cornelia is now close enough to read Sheriff Tate's thoughts, and he certainly has discovered a lot of details that would have come in handy earlier today.

"Better late than never, cotton ball," Orwin commented, still holding the side of his neck. The injury wasn't bad, but my premonition could still play out. The cabin in my vision might actually be our safety net. "That's exactly what I was thinking, Lou. Emily is who shot Knox, and she's the one he is hunting now."

"How do you know all that?" Sheriff Tate demanded, her gaze darting between us and the dark abyss beyond to search for any sign of her daughter. I held up my hands, though not for the reason Sheriff Tate believed was my acquiesce. "You're one of them, aren't you? I didn't believe Emily, but it all makes sense now. You people *are* vampires. What have you done with my daughter?"

Oh, dear! I'm guessing now might be another good time to retreat and regroup.

I instantly lifted my hand and all but tossed Sheriff Tate one way and her weapon the other. We had no idea if Knox had neutralized Emily, but it was best not to take any chances.

"Run!" I yelled, using all my energy to make sure that Sheriff Tate wouldn't be retrieving her weapon anytime soon. By the time I'd unleashed all the energy from my body, her firearm was buried in a snowbank on the other side of the road. The sheriff would take a while to find it, so I was close behind Orwin and Piper within seconds. "Go, go, go!"

Another growl from Knox, somewhere to the left of us, practically vibrated the trees as we continued to run through the dense woods. It was shortly followed by a shrill scream that could only have come from Emily. Terror froze my blood in a way that the weather couldn't, and I brought myself up short.

You need to trust your werewolf, Miss Lilura. He didn't spend all that time in that cave continuously changing into his intimidating form for no reason. Mr. Emeric is in complete control of his hunting instincts, as we must do the same with our survival instincts. Now get those buttocks moving, dear hexed one. We have no time to waste!

Chapter Sixteen

ORWIN BURST THROUGH the abandoned cabin's front door, holding the side of his neck just as he'd done in my premonition. It was nighttime versus daytime, and his injury wasn't nearly enough to cause death, but that might not have been the case had Pearl not had the wherewithal to be in tune with our surroundings.

No need to stroke my ego, dear hexed one. We're all safe, and that is what matters. Would you care to see if this place has electricity?

"Pearl, I don't know what to say," Orwin began as we all followed him inside. He tried the switch by the door. Thankfully, a small light came on that had been positioned on the entryway table. I quickly shut the door, completely willing to spend the night here. We needed time to regroup, anyway. "You saved my life."

Did I? It was in the spur of the moment, so don't think for a second that I won't continue to poke fun about your wacky conspiracy theories. Some are seriously over the top.

"Knox wouldn't hurt Emily," Piper said softly while Orwin and Pearl continued to banter. "He'll be here soon enough once he retraces our steps."

I continued to search the cabin for any signs that someone might return at any moment, but found none whatsoever. There were no curtains on the windows, which meant we needed to shut off the light before someone spotted the golden hue from afar. Honestly, I just needed to keep busy. All I kept replaying in my mind was the sound of Emily's screams that seemed to echo forever inside these woods.

I'm sure the sheriff's daughter was quite fraught at the sight of a massive lycanthrope straight out of a horror movie. Speaking of which, we might want to toss around some excuses to give the residents on top of this mountain while we're waiting around in this abandoned cabin. I vote for an alien invasion. I'm sure we can spin the story in our favor.

"You don't need to shut off the light," Piper said as I went to flip off the switch. She'd set down Orwin's laptop that she held onto all this time, along with removing her body purse. She closed her eyes and held up her hands as she began to softly chant a spell. Orwin and Pearl had stopped razzing one another to give Piper silence in her concentration. Once she'd finished the incantation, she smiled brightly. "See? All done. No one will see the light shining through the windows."

Mr. Emeric should be here momentarily. He can explain his run-in with the sheriff's daughter, and thus offer some details that may help us in this endeavor.

"I don't think Emily Tate is going to buy that the werewolf she encountered was from a different planet."

Orwin took the scarf Piper had pulled from her purse and pressed the soft fabric against his neck. While there were drying droplets of blood running down to his collarbone, it was clear to see that his injury had just been a graze. "We need to come up with something better than that."

"What about a gas leak?" Piper asked, pushing Orwin's hand out of the way so she could get a better look at his wound. The premonition clock had to have gone past the timeframe by now, so we could breathe a little easier. With that said, there were still quite a few loose ends to tie up. "We did it, Orwin. See? I knew all along that you would be okay."

Piper and Orwin continued to exchange reasons that could explain a werewolf and a witch to the only law enforcement in this town. Their distraction afforded me the time I needed to sort through everything that had occurred within the last twenty-four hours.

I can help you with that, dear hexed one. I just so happened to be listening in on every thought Mr. Cornelia entertained while I was glued to his side. Loads of conspiracy theories in that noggin.

Pearl had gracefully jumped up on the rickety side table next to the window while I stared out into the darkness looking for any sign of Knox. I truly believed that Knox could control his rage while in his changed form, but what if Emily Tate had tried to attack him? What if she'd set off a chain reaction that had Knox acting on instinct? The results could be fatal.

"I thought back to this morning's encounter at the diner, and Orwin hadn't been within six feet of Emily Tate. She'd stayed at her table the entire time without giving away that she, too, had been hunting Jerry." My summarization meant that Jerry was still in trouble. I debated leaving Orwin and Piper here at the cabin. It might take me twenty minutes to head back to Hal's house, but I still might be able to warn the couple that they needed to come with me until the storm passed and Emily received notification that the bounty on Jerry's head had been lifted. "I'll give Knox a few more minutes. If he doesn't show up, I'll have no choice but to head out into this storm to make the trek back to Hal's place. We gave Cassandra our word that we would protect Jerry."

That we did, dear hexed one. The storm is picking up, though. I fear the only hunter left for us to worry about is Miss Emily Tate. Should our resident werewolf be able to neutralize her, Miss Saruman and her beau will be safe until morning. A piece of the puzzle that Mr. Cornelia was able to fit nicely into place was that the sheriff's daughter had deviously made sure that Frank Palisade's crossbow was visible to those who bothered to look at his bag.

"Emily had wanted the upper hand over Jerry, so she'd made it so that he thought Frank Palisade was the lone threat." It had been a very strategic move on Emily's part. I gave her kudos for thinking outside the box, but that didn't explain Frank's murder. I was confident that Jerry and Cassandra had nothing to do with the hunter's demise. Did that mean we had another player on top of this mountain? "We've confirmed that the key players are nowhere near here, so who killed Frank Palisade?"

"Emily." Orwin might have been conversing with Piper, but he'd been listening to every word that Pearl and I had been exchanging for the last minute. With a cabin this small, it didn't surprise me that he was able to overhear our conversation. "I was able to read Sheriff Tate's thoughts right before you all but threw her across the road. Apparently, Frank confronted Emily inside the bar. He'd figured out who had messed with his hunting gear, and also that she'd planned on getting that bounty for herself. She hadn't wanted anyone to overhear them, so they went upstairs to his room. One thing led to another, and she apparently killed him in self-defense. That's the story that Emily told her mother."

"So, Sheriff Tate arrested Jerry to throw the police off Emily's trail?" I asked, watching the snow come down heavier than before. I wasn't sure I'd even be able to trek back to Hal's place in this type of snowstorm. "I didn't take the sheriff as that type of person."

"The memories I saw from Tate might have taken place after Jerry's arrest." Orwin adjusted the scarf a little tighter around his neck, using it as a makeshift bandage. It would have to do until we could get ahold of a first aid kit. He sank into the beat-up old couch that had seen better days, coughing when a layer of dust puffed up into the chilly air. "I'm believe they had been talking in the sheriff's office."

"I'm sure Sheriff Tate didn't believe a word her daughter said in that moment," Piper said, giving the sheriff the benefit of the doubt. "I mean, can you imagine being told that vampires existed when you had no idea about the supernatural realm in general? Emily was lucky that her mother didn't call the loony bin."

Piper hadn't joined Orwin on the couch, but instead walked over to the small cabinet against a sink that served as part of the kitchen area. She was probably searching for a first aid kit.

"Pearl, you're awfully quiet," I murmured, reluctantly deciding that I wouldn't be able to make it back to Hal's place in this weather. If the groans of the cabin were anything to go by, the gust of winds had picked up speed once again. "Anything you want to add?"

I'd like to add that I'm glad we made it to the safety of this cabin with everyone's lives intact. We were able to thwart your premonition, clear up any misunderstandings we may have had with Miss Saruman, and remove the bounty on her beau's head. There is the pesky problem of the sheriff knowing about vampires. Given that her daughter is a hunter, it may have been a forgone conclusion. The truth was bound to come out at some point. All in all, I'd say this current case was a success, dear hexed one.

"Cassandra can't help us, though," Piper pointed out, though not without a solution. She was an optimist at heart, even though she'd come up empty on the search for a first aid kit. "We'll have to start searching for another medium. My coven didn't have anyone with that specialty, but I'm sure there's one out there somewhere."

I appreciated that Pearl had pointed out all the successes we'd had in the past twenty-four hours. We'd done what we'd set out to do, which was to save Orwin's life. Hearing it said aloud allowed me to finally truly breathe, but I wouldn't relax my guard in the least until Knox walked through the door to the cabin.

Then you'll be happy to know that your wish is about to come true, dear hexed one.

I turned from the window upon hearing Pearl's declaration, taking a step toward the only entrance in the cabin. I was brought to a complete halt when the door finally flung open wide to reveal Knox...and he wasn't alone.

Another twist I didn't see coming, Miss Lilura. By chance, do you know how to properly strip search someone?

Chapter Seventeen

"DO I WANT to know how you convinced Emily Tate that you aren't a threat to her?" I murmured, knowing full well how our voices carried throughout this tiny cabin. "After all, she did see you in werewolf form."

"First off, I can be very charming," Knox replied, tossing a grin my way. We were currently sitting on the bed in the corner, allowing Sheriff Tate and her daughter to have the couch. Orwin had moved to the chair, and Piper was using the arm to hoist herself up. The four of them were having a serious conversation about the supernatural realm, and how everyone just wanted to live in harmony. "Second, I didn't change fully. Only enough to scare Emily into listening to what I had to say. I'm pretty sure she was just too shocked to move, but I was still able to convince the two of them to ride out the storm here."

An hour had passed since Knox had shown up at the cabin door with Sheriff Tate and her daughter in tow. Knox had gone about getting us some firewood that had been in a box out back with a tarp wrapped around it, providing us with a good heat source for the remainder of our time there. Piper had raided the lone cupboard and discovered coffee grounds and a pot, for which she was able to make us coffee using the flames in the hearth.

Pearl would have to wait until morning to get her spot of warm cream.

Don't remind me. By the way, that wasn't a gust of wind you just heard. It was the rumbling in my stomach.

"You realize that if I'd changed fully into my were-wolf form, I wouldn't be wearing any clothes right now, right?"

I so wasn't answering that question.

Perhaps you should, dear hexed one.

I took the safest route, which was to discuss our next move.

I might need to adjust my knock-knock jokes to include a bit of encouragement in the romance department. Duly noted, Miss Lilura. You're a slow starter.

It was a really good thing that Knox couldn't hear Pearl.

"Professor Weaver is the only loose thread in this scenario," I pointed out after clearing my throat. We'd all been able to remove our jackets. Seeing as we were pretty much stuck here for the duration of the storm, I scooted back on the bed until I could lean my shoulders against the wall behind us. "I mean, other than the fact that good ol' Uncle Hal has no place to live. Hopefully, someone will offer him a place to stay until he and Jerry can rebuild their home. With that said, we might need to drive back to Minnesota. Professor Weaver put a hit out on one of his former students. That can't go without some consequences."

I took a sip of the black coffee, grateful when the warmth spread throughout my body. A jolt of caffeine would be good right about now.

I'm glad to see you enjoying your beverage of choice, dear hexed one.

I couldn't help but lift my mug in salute, unable to prevent the smirk that graced my lips.

You find my plight amusing, but I will have you know that I've deduced you have a very dry sense of humor. I might need to switch off knock-knock jokes entirely to some appropriate English humor.

"I'm sure Cassandra can handle the professor," Knox said, lifting his own coffee cup to his lips. After he'd taken a fortifying sip, he motioned toward Emily. "Do you think she'll stop hunting?"

"Piper can be very convincing," I reminded him wryly, thinking about Knox's personality change. Technically, he was still quite intimidating and only spoke when he had something to say. It was the flirting I needed to get used to, because there was no room in our lives for anything but a partnership at this point. We had two curses to cure, and no time to waste. "I feel for Jerry and his brother. They never asked for their lives to be turned upside down, let alone to be targeted for assassination."

"Hmmm," Knox hummed, the vibrations from his body washing over mine. "That sounds oddly familiar."

We continued to sit in silence, listening in on the conversation taking place between the others. The blazing fire continued to crackle and pop, giving off welcome heat that chased away the cold that seemed to have settled into my bones. The cabin wasn't as comfortable as the RV, but we were safe.

Orwin was alive, and that was all that mattered. He caught my eye, mouthing a silent *thank you*. I nodded back, knowing full well I didn't have to tell him we were all in this together. He'd come with me on this journey, and his secret was still safe with me, tucked away in the corner recesses of my mind where Pearl wouldn't have access to it. When he was ready, he would share his reason for accompanying me on this journey with the others. In the meantime, I would take this night of reprieve given to us and hope that I didn't experience another premonition.

"My shoulder makes for a great pillow," Knox murmured, leaning his head back against the wall and closing his eyes. I resisted the urge to run my fingertips over his five o'clock shadow. We were partners, and I would do well to remember that. "We might as well get some rest. Who knows what tomorrow will bring."

May I point out a bright spot, dear hexed one?

I did my best to stop myself from smiling, knowing full well that Pearl was going to tell me about this bright spot even if I'd said no. I also went ahead and used Knox's shoulder against my own better advice. He was right. It made for a better pillow than the hard wall behind us, and I needed to be ready for whatever tomorrow brought our way.

Our own Mr. Emeric was cursed with lycanthropy. A curse that would have bitten sour grapes had it been one with fangs and the need to drink blood to survive. Imagine wondering if he was going to bite you every time you turned your back, dear hexed one.

Pearl always did manage to point out the bright spots in our cases, and she wouldn't be wrong this time, either. Having our very own werewolf on the team had proved useful many times already.

Now that you're seeing things my way, I should point out that I finally understand our alien hunter's need to search for extraterrestrial life. I will do my best to corral my witticism regarding his conspiracy theories, though difficult it may be. If I was a descendent from Ammeline Letty Romilda, I'd want an escape plan, too. No worries, dear hexed one. I shall reserve my next knock-knock joke until tomorrow. After all, I do have impeccable manners.

~ THE END ~

Thank you so much for joining Lou and the gang as they continue to solve supernatural mysteries! There are more magical whodunits in their future, and you can find out more about *Curse Me Under the Mistletoe* below…

kennedylayne.com/curse-me-under-the-mistletoe.html

Curses and kisses are stirring up a cloud of fresh snowflakes this holiday season in the latest installment in the Hex on Me Mysteries by USA Today Bestselling Author Kennedy Layne…

Delicious peppermint candy canes, a mug of creamy hot chocolate, and a deadly curse all seem to be connected in the next mystery that Lou and the gang unravel just in time for the winter solstice. Not for the first time, another one of Lou's premonitions ends up with a dead body. This time, there seems to be a seasonal twist…in the form of a very special type of mistletoe.

Grab your earmuffs and scarves if you want to help Lou and the gang solve this latest whodunit in a magical winter wonderland this holiday season!

Books by Kennedy Layne

Hex on Me Mysteries
If the Curse Fits
Cursing up the Wrong Tree
The Squeaky Ghost Gets the Curse
The Curse that Bites
Curse Me Under the Mistletoe

Paramour Bay Mysteries
Magical Blend
Bewitching Blend
Enchanting Blend
Haunting Blend
Charming Blend
Spellbinding Blend
Cryptic Blend
Broomstick Blend
Spirited Blend

Office Roulette Series
Means (Office Roulette, Book One)
Motive (Office Roulette, Book Two)
Opportunity (Office Roulette, Book Three)

Keys to Love Series
Unlocking Fear (Keys to Love, Book One)
Unlocking Secrets (Keys to Love, Book Two)
Unlocking Lies (Keys to Love, Book Three)
Unlocking Shadows (Keys to Love, Book Four)
Unlocking Darkness (Keys to Love, Book Five)

ABOUT THE AUTHOR

First and foremost, I love life. I love that I'm a wife, mother, daughter, sister... and a writer.

I am one of the lucky women in this world who gets to do what makes them happy. As long as I have a cup of coffee (maybe two or three) and my laptop, the stories evolve themselves and I try to do them justice. I draw my inspiration from a retired Marine Master Sergeant that swept me off of my feet and has drawn me into a world that fulfills all of my deepest and darkest desires. Erotic romance, military men, intrigue, with a little bit of kinky chili pepper (his recipe), fill my head and there is nothing more satisfying than making the hero and heroine fulfill their destinies.

Thank you for having joined me on their journeys...

Email: kennedylayneauthor@gmail.com

Facebook: facebook.com/kennedy.layne.94

Twitter: twitter.com/KennedyL_Author

Website: www.kennedylayne.com

Newsletter:
www.kennedylayne.com/aboutnewsletter.html